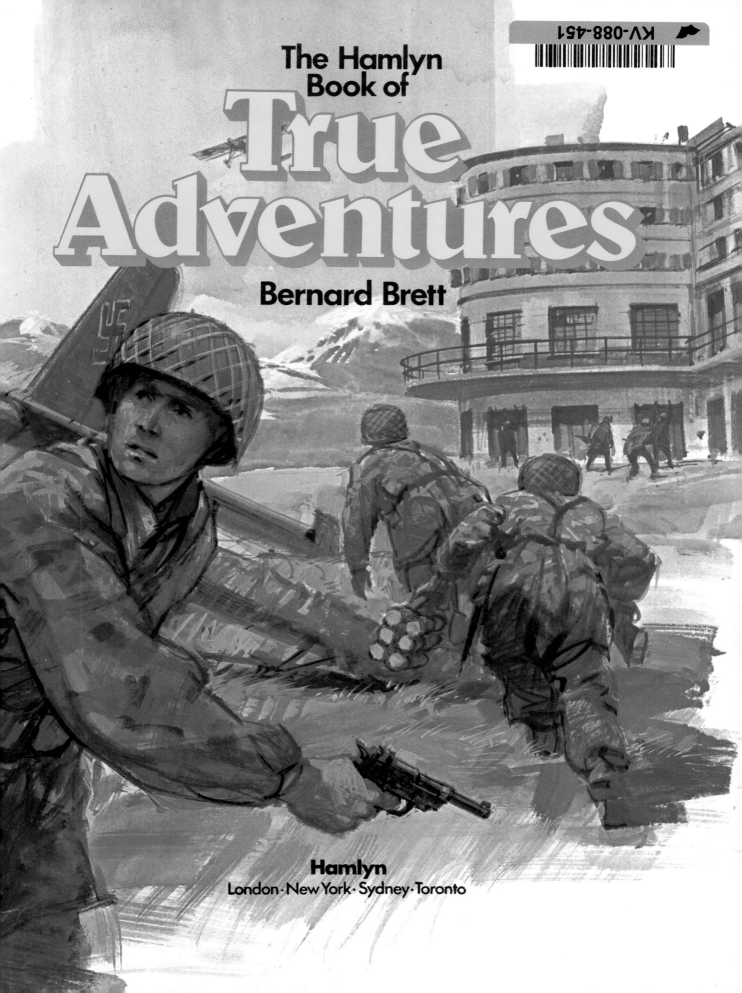

The Hamlyn Book of True Adventures

Bernard Brett

Hamlyn
London · New York · Sydney · Toronto

Contents

Illustrated by:

**Peter Archer   Mike Bell   Mike Codd
Mike Cole   Brian Evans   Donald Harley   Peter Morgan
Ted Osmond   Pat Owen   Michael Turner**

Acknowledgements

The illustration on page 136 is reproduced by permission of Her Majesty's Stationery Office.

Photographs

Austrian National Tourist Office, London 148–149; Barratt's Photo Press Ltd., London 154; Commander A. Fraccaroli, Pura 116 inset, 120 inset; Crown Copyright 136; French Embassy, London 57 inset; Hamlyn Group Picture Library 99 bottom right inset, 134; Imperial War Museum, London 99 top right inset; Nan Kivell Collection, National Library of Australia, Canberra 67 bottom right, 74–75; Louisville and Nashville Railroad Company, Kentucky 44–45; Mansell Collection, London 62–63, 66, 67, top left, 67 top right, 78–79, 113 inset, 114, 115, 139; National Portrait Gallery, London 138; Janus Piekalkiewicz Bild-archiv, Overath–Heiligenhaus 11 inset; Popperfoto, London 34; Royal Geographical Society, London 101, 102, 104–105, 106–107, 109, 110, 111; Z.E.F.A. – D Baglin 64.

To
Jamie
With Love & Best Wishes
Tom, Jill & James
x x x

First published 1978 by
The Hamlyn Publishing Group Limited
London · New York · Sydney · Toronto
Astronaut House, Feltham, Middlesex, England

ISBN 0 600 30357 8

Printed and bound in Great Britain by
Morrison & Gibb Ltd, London and Edinburgh.

Introduction

Truth is ever stranger than fiction as this collection of true adventure stories shows. Covering a wide field, they have been selected to show how men and women, caught in spine-chilling situations, have faced up to danger and difficulty. Sometimes they win through, other times they fail, often with tragic results; but they have one thing in common, the indomitable will to survive and succeed. Many of them conjure up hair-raising pictures; imagine grop-

ing through the murky waters of Alexandria harbour sitting astride an explosive-packed 'pig', or crawling along the wing of a bomber flying at 3,000 metres with a howling slipstream trying to tear you from your precarious hold. Yet some of the people in these stories did just that and then incredibly came back for more.

A few of the adventures end in tragedy, often through mistake or error of judgement, as in the case of HMS submarine *Thetis*. A torpedo tube open to the sea, a sudden rush of water and a hundred odd men are trapped a few heart-breaking metres from the surface: would they have been rescued had they been carrying only their normal complement? How much did the unfortunate choice of Burke as leader affect the outcome of the ill-fated expedition to cross the Australian outback? It is easy to criticise with hindsight but no doubt it seemed the right thing to do at the time.

Other stories tell of feats of daring as exemplified by the swashbuckling Skorzeny's rescue of Mussolini, or the kidnapping of a German general from under the noses of 30,000 of his men by two young British officers, one barely twenty and the other only eighteen. The grit and determination of a lone woman flier or a man trapped for thirteen days beneath an avalanche; the final assault on Everest; all these widely different situations contain the ingredients that go to make up a good adventure 'yarn'.

9

CHAPTER 1

The Kidnapping of General Kreipe

*Disguised as peasants,
they left straight away to contact
the nearest radio operator; Cairo must be
informed that the commando unit
was sailing into a trap.*

The four men had to shout to make themselves heard above the roar of the aircraft's engines. Not that they had much to say to each other; they were far too busy turning over in their minds the desperate mission on which they were embarking. What chance, if any, had it of succeeding? For the last hour they had sat huddled together, cold and miserable, as the Wellington bomber buffeted its way through bad weather across the Mediterranean from Bardia. The only grudging gesture towards comfort were canvas seats bolted to the deck.

It was the night of 4 February 1944. Their destination – Crete. Their mission to kidnap General Wilhelm Müller, whose brutal regime had earned him the undying hatred of the Cretan population. The kidnapping had been planned not only to lower the morale and prestige of the German occupation forces on the island, but also to mislead the German General Staff as to the intentions of the Allies in the Balkans.

Patrick Leigh Fermor jumping alone into the 'valley of the thousand windmills'. Inset: a contemporary photograph

At first glance, the men in the Wellington made an unlikely-looking team. Their leader, Patrick Leigh Fermor, was barely twenty years old but had already reached the rank of major. As his second-in-command he had chosen Captain Stanley Moss who was younger – only eighteen. Making up the commando unit were their two swarthy companions, Manoli Paterakis and Georgi Tyrakis, who were Greek agents of the British Special Operations Executive, or the SOE.

Below them lay the island of Crete – 260 kilometres long and 60 kilometres wide. Its steeply rising mountain range was riddled with hundreds of caves which offered admirable shelter to the partisans, operating under British instructors.

'Stand by to jump!' came the order. A green light flashed on. As the jump-master pulled back the door the sound of the engines became deafening. The parachutes had been hooked up and the youthful leader of the expedition crouched in the doorway ready to be the first out. Patches of mist were making it difficult for the pilot to locate the jumping-off area which was called the Lasithi Plain. Set in the middle of the desolate mountain region, the plain was known locally as the 'valley of the thousand windmills.'

At the first gap in the mist, there was a tap on Leigh Fermor's shoulder and he was out, dropping like a stone until he felt a violent jerk as his chute opened. Then he was floating gently down towards the packed windmills and the partisan reception committee waiting for him below. Anxiously, he looked up over his shoulder for signs of the others, but they were nowhere in sight. A heavy mist had fallen and despite several attempts, the pilot was unable to drop the other three men.

Meanwhile, the partisans took Leigh Fermor to a peasant hut. He waited there all the following night, for the arrival of his fellow commandos and the provisions which had remained in the aircraft. In fact, it was several weeks before another attempt could be made, and that failed because the heavy ground fog obscured the partisans' signal-lights. Once again the pilot had to turn back. After two long months of waiting, Leigh Fermor received the news that his companions would be landing from a British motor launch on the southern coast of the island. So, accompanied by a group of partisans, he set out to meet them.

After two days of arduous and often dangerous climbing, they arrived at a peak overlooking the coast. They scrambled down the last few kilometres to the beach and settled down behind some rocks to await the motor launch. Only a few weeks before, this beach had been littered with landmines, but heavy breakers and herds of sheep had gradually detonated them all. The only danger came from the German coastal guards who were posted a distance of two kilometres away at each end of the beach.

A dark shape was sighted drifting towards the shore: A beam of light flashed a brief signal from the beach, and within a few minutes a dinghy had landed the three agents. After exchanging enthusiastic greetings, the newcomers were told that General Müller, the object of their mission, had left the island two days previously. Their new target was General Heinrich Kreipe who had just been transferred to Crete from the Russian Front. So, travelling by night, they marched across the mountains in the direction of the village of Kastamonitza, where they were to be lodged with a local peasant family. Just as dawn was breaking they came to a place behind the ridge of a hill where

The other commandos arriving by motor launch. The Germans mined many beaches in occupied territories to prevent any possibility of invasion by Allied troops

The second night's march took them to Skonia where they were welcomed by a partisan family. They sat down to a table richly laden with food, wine and Ouzo, a strong, raw spirit. Following an old Greek custom in which everybody drinks whenever a member of the company raises his glass, they soon turned into a noisy party. One by one, the villagers trooped in to greet the agents. The two village policemen came along too, to offer their services.

they remained for the whole of the first day. They ate a hasty meal first, for they were weary after five hours heavy marching, and then they slept till dusk.

After a short sleep the men were off again by ten o'clock at night and on their way to Kastamonitza, which they reached by daybreak. Their reception here was very different to that at Skonia. They ate well but there was very little drinking and the shutters were tightly closed as members of the family mounted constant guard in the yard outside. No wonder! Kastamonitza was crawling with German soldiers from a convalescent home that had recently been set up in the village.

The next day, Micky Akaumianos, the chief SOE agent in Crete, arrived by motor bus from the capital, Heraklion, bringing with him forged papers and passports. He was to take Leigh Fermor back with him to Heraklion the following day to spy out the land and devise a plan for the kidnapping. Moss and a group of partisans set off to establish a headquarters in the hills above the village.

Micky and Leigh Fermor were disguised as peasants and, surrounded by farm produce and livestock, they passed unnoticed in the crowded bus. They reached Heraklion without having to show their papers and then walked the seven kilometres to Knossos, where the German commander of the island had his residence. The sight of Villa Ariadne, built by the archaeologist Arthur Evans and now the residence of General Kreipe, was a daunting one. It was surrounded by heavy barbed wire and it had several guard posts. There was no doubt that the efficient-looking sentries who patrolled the grounds knew how to use the machine-pistols they carried. Leigh Fermor realised that it would be madness to try a direct assault on the villa. They would have to think of another way – a way that would surprise the enemy.

The two men stayed with Micky's parents, who lived in a farm attached to the Villa Ariadne. From there they were able to keep an eye on the villa, noting the General's movements and the routine of the guards. For a fortnight they continued to watch, often chatting with visiting soldiers from General Kreipe's establishment. One reason for Leigh Fermor being picked for the mission was that he spoke fluent Greek and German. Micky Akaumianos writes, 'We kept to the vicinity of our house and watched the General's habits and the comings and goings at the villa. We spent some nights outside the locality, in order to test all the details of our plan, and also made contact with some of the General's military staff and found out as much as possible about his movements.' Their plan was to kidnap Kreipe when he returned at night from his military headquarters or from the officers' mess at Ano Archanes, which was twenty kilometres from the Villa Ariadne.

Moss and his party had reached their hideout – a cave on a mountain slope high above Kastamonitza – after a march of several hours. It offered them a perfect view of the surrounding countryside. The cave was only a few metres wide and little more than a metre high, but it sheltered them from the biting mountain wind and a stream nearby provided them with fresh water. As well as their provisions, they had gifts of wine, goat's milk cheese and milk brought to them by shepherds – wild-looking men draped in sheep skins.

Leigh Fermor and Akaumianos joined Moss and his party in the cave on Easter Sunday and presented their detailed plan. The kidnapping was to take place at a hairpin-bend, where the road from Ano Archanes joined the Knossos – Heraklion road. This bend was so sharp that any car from Ano Archanes had to slow down to a walking pace. The plan was that Leigh Fermor and Moss, wearing German military police uniforms, supplied by Akaumianos from some mysterious source, would set up a road-block to stop the General's car. They would then bundle him into the back and bluff their way through the enemy control posts. Moss would drive the car and Leigh Fermor would sit next to him wearing the General's cap. The Opel would be abandoned in the mountains and they would complete their journey to the south coast on foot, where a British motor launch would take them off. This simple plan depended on split-second timing and a great deal of luck, in order to succeed.

It was agreed with Bourdzalis, a guerilla leader, that he and his men would assist in the kidnapping by dealing with any German patrols that might stray into the area. These partisans – an undisciplined band of wild mountain men – carried rusty rifles that had probably seen service with their fathers.

That night, the men left the cave for the last time and made their way to Skalani, a village five kilometres from the spot chosen for the kidnapping. Bourdzalis and his men were housed in the broken-down hut of a wine-grower, but they could not be persuaded to keep under cover and insisted on roaming about the countryside. They were soon noticed by local peasants, so, reluctantly, Leigh Fermor had to dispense with their services before they alerted the Germans.

It was 9.30pm on 26 April 1944. Leigh Fermor and Moss were crouching together in a ditch alongside the hairpin-bend on the Ano Archanes road. They were both dressed as German military police and had even given one another a typically German haircut. Several hundred metres up the road, Micky Akaumianos and his partisans lay in wait. It was their job to warn the Englishmen of Kreipe's approach and deal with any traffic that might come along the road at the time of the

Patrick Leigh Fermor and Micky Akaumianos, disguised as peasants and sitting amongst market produce, pass unnoticed in the crowded local bus

ambush. A length of string stretched between the two parties. It was attached to a small bell beside the two Englishmen and made a crude but effective warning system. Leigh Fermor and Moss were both nervous and tense and they jumped when the bell suddenly began to ring. In a flash, they had leapt from the ditch and had set up their red lamps and the halt sign.

General Heinrich Kreipe had had a busy day visiting his widely scattered units, and he had spent a pleasant evening relaxing in the officers' club. Now he felt pleasantly tired as he lolled in the back seat of his Opel. A machine-pistol lay on the seat beside him. He later wrote: 'Suddenly a red light appeared in the darkness in front of us, approximately on the bend.'

'Shall I stop, herr General?' asked his chauffeur, Albert.

Kreipe saw two lance-corporals of the military police standing in the middle of the road, waving their arms. 'Stop,' he said to Albert.

The older of the two lance-corporals demanded to see his travel permit.

Kreipe is known to have said, 'Don't know about that.'

'In that case, the password please.'

'Then I did something foolish,' the General goes on. 'I got out of the car and said, "What unit are you? Don't you know your General?" Leigh Fermor, in his German disguise, said, "General, you are a prisoner of war in British hands".'

Kreipe made a dive for his machine-pistol, but was quickly overpowered by Georgi and Manoli then trussed up and thrown into the back of the car. The two SOE men jumped in after him and crouched behind the front seat, Georgi holding a dagger to the German's throat. Kreipe did not doubt that the Greek would use it if he attempted to escape, or called out. Moss took the wheel, and with Leigh Fermor beside him, wearing Kreipe's cap, he slipped the car into first gear and they skidded off in the direction of Heraklion. Akaumianos and his men, with the chauffeur Albert, set off in the opposite direction.

The kidnapping of General Kreipe is accomplished very smoothly and according to plan, but the trickiest part of the operation is still to come

The General, many years older than his kidnappers, is unable to maintain the gruelling pace, and has to be carried to the next refuge

The kidnapping itself had gone off without a hitch, but the trickiest part was still to come. They had to bluff their way past the German control posts and road blocks. They sped past the palace of Knossos and the Villa Ariadne, to the outskirts of Heraklion. There to their intense relief the officer of the guard saluted them and stepped aside, convinced of the authenticity of the staff car flying the General's pennant. As Kreipe himself later said, 'I knew that in Heraklion there were several control posts – only one of them called out to us!'

At the Rethumon cross-roads Kreipe was hustled out of the car and marched off to Anoya by Moss and the two Greeks. Leigh Fermor took over the wheel and drove the Opel two kilometres down the road to the beach. From this point a British submarine had recently shelled the airfield at Heraklion. He abandoned the car, leaving in it a letter in English and

German, which said that British commandos had kidnapped General Kreipe without assistance from the Cretan population, and that the General was on his way to Cairo. To add colour he left a green commando beret, some Player's cigarette stubs and an Agatha Christie novel. He then set off to rendezvous with Moss in Anoya. Next day the BBC Overseas Service was to broadcast, 'General Kreipe is on his way to Cairo.'

The General's staff at the villa became anxious as dawn approached and Kreipe had

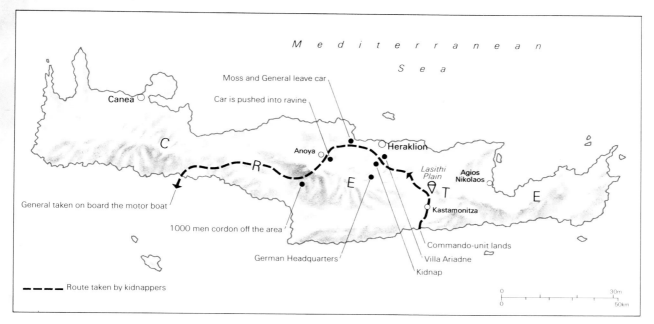

Route taken by kidnappers

still not returned. The alarm was finally given when it was confirmed that he had left the officers' club at 9pm the previous night. The 30,000 troops on Crete were immediately thrown into an island-wide search. Fieseler Storch scouting aircraft combed the mountains and other known haunts of the partisans. A leaflet was hastily run-off and distributed throughout Crete. It read:

To all inhabitants of Crete
Last night bandits kidnapped the German General Kreipe. He is being held some-where in the mountains. His whereabouts cannot be unknown to the population. If, therefore, the General is not released within three days, all the rebel villages in the vicinity of Heraklion will be razed to the ground. The severest measures will be taken against the civilian population.

Later in the day the abandoned Opel was discovered by the sea. The letter was read, and this, in conjunction with the BBC broadcast, convinced the Germans that they were too late and next morning they called off the search. Later, German Intelligence on the island received a report from one of their agents that Kreipe *was* still on Crete being held captive by partisans. Once again the hunt was on, but this time with redoubled vigour.

Moss and his party made for Anoya where they were to meet Leigh Fermor; the going was

rugged, as a rueful General Kreipe writes. 'For the next few days we walked through very rough country – at night, or at dusk. During the daylight hours we stayed in caves or hide-outs in the forest; the ground was rocky. It was very difficult indeed, there were of course no paths.'

A warning beacon flared up in the nearby mountains as they approached Anoya, so Moss decided to make straight for the tumbledown hut where Leigh Fermor was waiting for them. Upon arrival Manoli was sent to the village to look round. They had hardly settled in and begun a meal when Manoli was back. The Germans had occupied Anoya and were fan-ning out to comb the surrounding hills. Once more they were on the move, struggling up a steep track in a southerly direction. After a gruelling two hour climb the General was on the point of collapse. Unable to continue, he slumped against a rock gasping for breath. Moss and Manoli, half-carrying Kreipe between them, continued until they arrived at a beehive-shaped stone shepherd's hut. Here they were fed by the shepherd on grilled mutton and wine. Later they lay by the open fire in the centre of the hut, eyes streaming from the smoke that failed to escape through the hole in the roof and tried to snatch a few hours sleep.

At daybreak, they steadily marched south to rendezvous with the four Cretans who were bringing the General's driver, Albert. In the

19

afternoon they sighted the others, but the driver was not with them. The Cretans told them that he had died from wounds sustained during the kidnapping. It was many years later before the truth came out: Albert had been stabbed to death by one of his captors and his body hidden beneath some rocks.

Caves and underground caverns are fairly numerous in Crete, but the beauties of this stalactite hideout are lost on the ever-vigilant kidnappers

They continued to travel south until on 30 April they reached the foot of Mount Ida, the highest mountain in Crete. The search had intensified and the kidnappers were constantly ducking behind rocks to avoid being seen by the searching Fieseler Storchs. Soon the mountain path became steeper and the going even more difficult. The kidnappers, hindered by the General who had to be half-carried, were forced to stop every few minutes. It was bitterly cold and at each step they skidded on layers of slippery ice. The freezing rain lashed their faces as they reached the snowline.

When at last, almost all in, they began to descend, the kidnappers sighted a warning beacon burning close by. The Germans, spread out in a thin line, were climbing systematically towards them. Their guide, a local shepherd, led them to a labyrinthine, stalactite cave.

They huddled together there throughout the night, with German search parties within earshot. Next morning, damp and cold, they crawled out into the early sunlight to be greeted by a messenger who brought the alarming news that German troops had been rushed south and were now stationed along the entire length of that coast. Immediately the party left, and after hours of further strenuous climbing they reached their next rendezvous point, another deserted shepherd's hut high on the slopes of Mount Ida. The partisan communication system never once let them down. As General Kreipe admits, 'I would like to mention, by the way, how excellently the communications network functioned. The partisans were always able to contact the kidnappers along their escape route to the south coast, and they were also constantly in touch with Cairo by radio.'

When they had been in the hut a few days another messenger arrived, this time with a radio message from Cairo – on one of the next four nights a commando unit would be landing on a south-coast beach to clear a passage for the kidnappers by force. They were only a few hours march from the coast. The journey would be downhill all the way. So they decided to set out in the early evening and make their way to a point above the escape beach, and there wait until the British commandos arrived. But before they could leave they received another message. The Germans had landed 200 troops in the area of the escape beach, completely sealing it off. It looked as if there must be an informer among the partisans. Disguised as peasants Leigh Fermor and Georgi left straight away to contact the nearest SOE radio operator; Cairo must be informed that the commando unit was sailing into a trap!

The kidnappers had decided that Moss and his party would take the General westwards along the coast to look for an unguarded beach. A message would then be sent to Leigh Fermor who would radio the new pick-up position to Cairo. Then news arrived that large German search-parties were combing the surrounding valleys, cutting off their route to the west. Moss and his party were forced to remain all that day and the next night in their hide-out. The situation was becoming desperate. They had to break out before they were completely surrounded. They did so and hours later reached Yerakari, a lonely village nestling at the foot of Mount Ida, after a nightmare journey playing hide and seek with the searching Germans. General Kreipe, out of condition and unused to strenuous exercise, was unable to go on. A mule was found for him and once more they climbed up steep mountain passes to a hut high above the village. Here they decided to wait for Leigh Fermor to contact them. Their position was beginning to look hopeless as the Germans closed in on them.

The next day Leigh Fermor and Georgi arrived with news of a lonely beach near Rodakino that appeared to be free from German troops. Cairo had been contacted and a motor

The mule procured for General Kreipe proves to be a very mixed blessing. On a treacherous mountain track the General is thrown, breaking his right shoulder and causing further problems for his kidnappers

launch had set out to pick them up – rendezvous time, 10pm on the night of 14 May. The kidnappers left their lonely hide-out and scrambled down the precipitous mountain tracks towards Rodakino. On a particularly treacherous stretch of loose shale, the mule stumbled, throwing the General. To add to their troubles they found that Kreipe had broken his right shoulder, and precious time was lost in patching him up. It was now touch and go whether or not they could reach the beach in time. The motor launch would wait for them, but not for long as the off-shore waters were heavily patrolled by German naval units and the launch would soon be discovered. They were forced to take a long route through the mountains to avoid the German net stretched along the coast. A partisan went ahead to warn them of any search parties.

*The General and his captors are taken safely off Crete
by British commandos to the port of Marsa Matruh*

Next evening found them stumbling down a steep cliff to the escape beach. The loose rubble underfoot made a silent approach impossible. Surely the noise of the pebbles bouncing down from rock to rock could be heard by every German for miles around? They heard the noise of motor launch engines but were they British or German? Then running feet crunched through shingle and they were faced by black-faced British commandos, armed to the teeth.

'Major Leigh Fermor? So you made it. Is that him?' Quickly they hurried into the dinghies and were whisked out to the launch. The commander had kept the engines running, and as soon as they were aboard, the course was set for Egypt. They bounced through the rough seas with their engines flat out, confident that nothing could catch them now.

Leigh Fermor could hardly believe he had succeeded in pulling off the almost impossible kidnapping, nor could the senior officers who met the party at the harbour of Marsa Matruh. Eventually General Kreipe found himself in a prisoner of war camp near Calgary in the Rocky Mountains of Canada, where he spent the rest of the war. But he seemed to have the last word. 'When we landed in Africa – at Marsa Matruh – the leader of the commandos, Colonel Bamfield, received me. He treated me correctly and was helpful in every way. But just imagine: for a whole fortnight I had had no clean handkerchief unless I first washed it in water!'

CHAPTER 2

The Man-Eaters of Tsavo

*The lions' methods
were so uncanny and so successful
that the superstitious workmen were
convinced that they were not animals
at all, but evil spirits in
lion's shape.*

When Colonel Patterson first saw Tsavo he thought it a dreary place. Mile after mile of stunted trees, whitish and leafless, thick undergrowth and 'wait-a-bit' thorn bushes stretched in every direction as far as the eye could see. Here and there a ridge of barren dark-red rock jutted above the 'nyika'. The sunstricken landscape was redeemed by a fast-flowing river, and the fringe of lofty green trees along its banks added a welcome touch of freshness to the grey wilderness.

The year was 1898 and the colonel, an engineer, had been sent to East Africa from England to assist in the construction of the Uganda Railway. His principal job was to build a railway bridge across the river and complete the permanent way (48 kilometres) each side of Tsavo. Supplies and labour, mainly Indian coolies, poured into Tsavo following his initial survey, and tented encampments were set up. At first the work went well and the sound of hammers and drills and the strident chatter of the labourers echoed happily through the jungle. Then began the reign of terror.

Patterson had been at Tsavo only a few days when a number of labourers mysteriously disappeared. His first thought was that the Indians, always thrifty with their wages, had been murdered for their money and their bodies buried in the jungle. But the other coolies solemnly assured Patterson that their friends had been carried off by two man-eating lions who were terrorising the district. Their man-stalking methods were so uncanny and so successful that the superstitious workmen were convinced that they were not animals at all, but

evil spirits in lion's shape. The story was soon put about that they were the angry spirits of two native chiefs, long since dead, who resented the railway coming across their land and who were taking this way of stopping its progress. Patterson was still inclined to believe that the missing workmen had been murdered for their money, but morale was at a low ebb and work output had dropped, so whatever the reason, the building of the railway was making slow progress. He had to act, and act quickly but what action could he take?

He was awakened in the middle of the night a few days later by his 'boy'. The Indian finally managed to get out his story although he was shaking with terror. One of the 'jemadars', or foremen, had been dragged from his tent and taken away and eaten. Patterson, still in his pyjamas, grabbed his ·303 rifle and rushed from his tent to the workmen's lines. A crowd of nervous Indians were huddled together outside

Patterson, running out of his tent, is too late to prevent yet another victim being seized by the blood-crazed animal

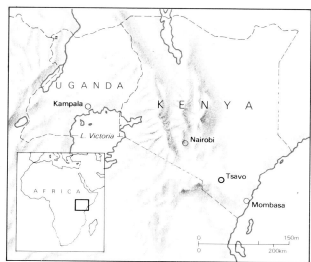

one of the tents listening to a colleague graphically describing the lion's attack. The 'jemadar,' a fine, powerful Sikh, who shared a tent with half-a-dozen other workmen, had always slept close to the open door. At about midnight a lion had suddenly thrust his head through the opening and seized Ungan Singh by the throat. The unfortunate 'jemadar' had screamed, 'choro' ('let go'), and grabbed at the lion's mane, but in a flash he was gone. The other Indians lay helpless, forced to listen to the dreadful struggle taking place outside. But the Sikh had no chance against the man-eater, and gradually his screams died away as he was dragged off into the jungle.

*The telegraph operator desperately tapping out a
signal for help – certainly the most unusual to be sent
from the tiny, country station*

Patterson was at first sceptical but was soon
convinced of the truth of the story when he
discovered the lion's pug marks plainly
visible in the sand. Furrows made by the madly
kicking heels of the 'jemadar' clearly showed
that he had been dragged into the jungle. The
colonel immediately set out to track down the
killer. He plunged into the jungle with a
companion, Captain Haslem. They found little
difficulty in following the route taken by the
lion, as pools of blood marked each spot at
which he had stopped with his victim. The
place where the body had been devoured was a
gruesome sight. Clearly, two lions had fought
for possession of the body.

They quickly buried the remains, but the
incident – his first experience of man-eaters –
made Patterson determined to rid the neigh-
bourhood of the brutes, and he vowed there
and then to hunt down any lion in the district.

For nine months the man-eaters terrorised
the railway. At first they were not always
successful in carrying off their victims, but as
time went on they became more daring and
resourceful and in December 1898 they succeeded in bringing railway work to a complete
standstill for three weeks.

It was towards the end of Patterson's stay in
Tsavo that one of the most horrifying and
grotesque attacks was made by a man-eater.
The lion had taken to haunting a little station
called Kima, and had made off with several
members of the railway staff. The daring
brute's timing was perfect; he always struck
when least expected, the instant that one of the
terrified station staff relaxed his vigilance.
Once, he leaped on to the roof of the station and,
growling and snarling tried to tear off the sheets
of corrugated iron. Immediately below him an
Indian telegraph operator cowered, frantically
tapping out a message to the Traffic Manager:
'Lion fighting with station. Send urgent
succour.' Although that night the killer was
unsuccessful, blood-stains on the roof from his
cut feet bore witness to just how hard he had
tried to get in.

28

In the nights that followed he had more success, carrying off an engine driver and several other victims. Incensed by the death of his colleague, another engine driver laid in wait for the man-eater. He hid in a large iron water tank, hoping to get a shot at the lion when it came marauding. The engine driver nodded off, but was jerked awake by the growls of the man-eater prowling round the station looking for a way in. Slowly the engine driver raised himself up and took aim. But the lion sensed his presence and with the cunning typical of the man-eaters of Tsavo, turned snarling, and leaped straight at the tank. The heavy iron tank swayed and then fell on its side and the would-be hunter looked like being the victim of the man-eater. The lion tried to drag out his victim with his paw by reaching through the hole in the top of the tank. Fortunately, the tank was too deep for the lion to reach the man who was crouching, half-paralysed with fear, at the bottom. In desperation he fired, and although his shot went wide the noise frightened away the lion.

Mr Ryall the superintendent of police, proposed to put a stop to the depredations of the man-eater once and for all. Accompanied by two of his friends, Mr Huebner and Mr Parenti, he travelled up to the lonely station in his inspection coach. This was detached from the train and shunted into a half-finished siding that had not been properly levelled, so the carriage listed badly as it rolled to a halt.

The would-be hunter, caught in his own trap, has a narrow escape from the cunning beast

That afternoon the three friends combed the adjacent jungle in search of the man-eater; they found plenty of pug marks, but they did not come across the brute himself. This did not surprise them for they knew that their best chance to get a shot at the lion was when it came marauding at night. They returned to the carriage, ate a leisurely dinner and afterwards sat up on guard. The usual night noises were heard in the jungle but nothing out of the normal occurred, although Huebner and Parenti remembered seeing what they believed to be two very bright glow-worms. This must have been the man-eater balefully studying their every move.

They had been watching for some time when Ryall suggested to his two friends that they should turn-in while he kept the first watch. They needed very little persuading for it had been a tiring day. Ryall offered the two berths in the carriage to his friends and Huebner immediately clambered into the high one above a table on one side of the carriage. The other berth was lower down on the opposite side of the carriage owing to the restricted space. Parenti said that he preferred a sleeping bag on the floor and lay down with his feet towards the sliding door leading into the carriage. Soon both men were asleep.

Why Ryall lay down in the other bunk will never be known. He may, after watching for some time, have come to the conclusion that the lion was not going to put in an appearance that night, and decided to turn-in. On the other hand he may have merely intended to make himself comfortable during a long watch and then dozed off. Whatever the reason, he had hardly nodded off before a black shadow slid silently from the edge of the jungle and made its way to the carriage. The man-eater, scenting his favourite prey, bounded up the two high steps leading to the little platform at the end of the carriage without a sound. It was an easy matter for him to thrust a paw through the gap in the partly closed door and shove it open. It slid noiselessly back on its brass runners. As soon as the killer had loped through the door, a combination of his extra weight and the tilt of the carriage caused the door to slide to; the lock snapped into place, leaving the man-eater shut in with the sleeping men.

Huebner, awakened by an agonised cry, leaped up in his berth in time to see Ryall frantically struggling with a snarling lion. Once inside the carriage the brute had sprung at once at Ryall, but to reach him he had to plant his feet on Parenti, asleep on the floor. Panic-stricken, Huebner climbed down from his berth. The only way of escape lay through a second sliding door leading to the servant's compartment. The enormous beast all but filled the cramped space and, in order to reach the door, Huebner had to jump on the man-eater's back. Incredibly, in the heat of the moment he did this and survived as the lion was too intent on his victim to pay any attention to him. He scrambled over the lion, hysterical with fear, and reached the door and safety. But, to his horror, it would not budge. The servants, hearing the roars of the blood-crazed lion in the next carriage, had threaded a turban through the handles of the door and were hanging on for dear life. Huebner's shouts made no impression on the Indians. They had no intention of opening the door with a man-eater on the other side. Huebner tore desperately at the door and managed to prise it open sufficiently for him to squeeze through. Immediately it was banged shut again and secured with turbans.

The other carriage was a shambles. Parenti, near to fainting, lay pinned down beneath the lion's hind legs, unable to move, while the brute tore at Ryall. The acrid stench of the man-eater filled the carriage and his shadow, thrown by the oil lamp, flickered across the wall. Parenti thought that in another minute he would go mad. Suddenly, there was a splintering crash and the whole carriage lurched violently sideways; the man-eater had broken through one of the windows, carrying off poor Ryall with him. Parenti was galvanised into life. He jumped through the window on the opposite side of the carriage and fled for the safety of the station buildings, unable to believe his miraculous escape. The whole episode had lasted for only a few minutes, yet for every interminable second, a lion, mad with blood-lust, had actually been standing on him.

The police superintendent's remains were found the next morning about 402 metres away in the bush. Shortly afterwards the man-eater responsible for this awful tragedy was caught in an ingenious trap set by one of the railway staff and was shot.

Incredibly, Huebner manages to escape by climbing over the lion's back. The beast is too intent upon his victim to notice the escaping man

CHAPTER 3

Impossible Mission

Behind their leader,
the tough assault troops checked
the firing mechanisms of their Schmeitzers,
loosened their commando knives and
made sure their grenades
were handy.

Above: *Il Duce at the height of his power before the fall of Tripoli in 1943.* Right: *Mussolini, an arrogant, overbearing man, in audience with King Victor Emmanuel is unable to get the normally timid monarch to reverse the Grand Council's decision to ask for his (Il Duce's) resignation*

Benito Mussolini, Il Duce, one time supreme dictator of Italy and her colonial empire, was a vainglorious, moody man, who had, for more than a decade, strutted across the pages of European history. All powerful and supported by the black-shirted Fascisti, he had led Italy into a disastrous war. His empire began to crumble as the war drew on, and when Tripoli fell early in 1943, his generals knew that the war was over for Italy and demanded that Il Duce sue for peace. Swayed by the mad dreams of his ally, Adolf Hitler, who had promised to reinstate him to his former glory Mussolini was for fighting on. At a stormy meeting in July 1943, the Grand Council of Italy voted by twenty eight votes to nineteen for his resignation and arrest. Count Ciano, Mussolini's son-in-law, was among those who voted for the dictator's arrest. His action was later to cost him his life, despite the hysterical pleadings of Mussolini's daughter, Edda.

The dictator had been seized quickly and hurried before the king of Italy who was to accept his resignation. Mussolini was confident that he could persuade the king to reverse the decision of the Grand Council for Victor Emmanuel, a little man, almost a midget, had always been terrified of Il Duce. This time the situation was changed. According to accounts, 'biting his nails nervously, and yellow-faced', the king had turned on Mussolini: 'You are the most hated man in the country,' he told him. No longer dictator, Mussolini was whisked into an ambulance and driven away.

For the next few weeks, he shuffled from prison to prison, a dejected and pathetic figure, until he eventually found himself in a former luxury hotel high in the Gran Sasso, the central mountain range of Italy. Here he was closely guarded by troops of the Alpine Regiment, who had sung during the North African desert campaign, 'Down with Mussolini, who murdered the Alpini.' They had orders to shoot him at the first sign of a rescue attempt, and they would clearly enjoy carrying out their orders, but unfortunately, as everyone knew, a rescue attempt was impossible. Who in their right mind would attempt such a thing?

Rumour had reached German Intelligence of Mussolini's whereabouts, and an army doctor was sent to examine the hotel on the pretext of using it as a temporary army hospital. He got no further than the foot of the mountain on which the hotel stood before he was turned back by a large group of Alpini. He concluded that Mussolini must be a prisoner on the mountain. Why else would a crack Italian regiment be posted to guard a remote hotel? Soon his news was on its way to Berlin.

The German General Staff were in a dilemma; they told Hitler the news, and added that unfortunately any rescue operation was out of the question. They had reckoned without the

A Luftwaffe transport plane carries Skorzeny to Hitler at Berchtesgaden

Führer. His face livid with rage, he turned on them and screamed, 'I don't care. Mussolini must be rescued.'

Hitler's outburst silenced his generals.

'But my Führer' – Field Marshal Keitel's protest dwindled away beneath the fixed stare of Germany's leader.

'Get him out, and get him out quickly!' ordered Hitler.

'Yes, my Führer. But how?'

'Send for Skorzeny.' As Hitler stormed out of the room his generals stared at each other in dismay. Skorzeny! Why he was not even a member of the regular Officer Corps.

Skorzeny, whose full title was SS Captain Otto Skorzeny, was the obvious, indeed the only choice to carry out such a mission. If anyone could rescue Mussolini he would be the man. Tough, ruthless, quick-witted, time and again he had proved himself to be the most dangerous single man in the Wehrmacht, with a string of successes as a leader of assault troops behind him. An Austrian, he had been a civil engineer until the outbreak of war; now he was rapidly becoming a legend, and more to the point, a firm favourite of the Führer. Reluctantly Keitel turned to his aide. 'Tell Hauptmann Skorzeny to report to me immediately.'

Twenty-four hours later, Otto Skorzeny, nearly two metres tall, clambered down from a

Luftwaffe transport plane. He couldn't understand why Keitel had sent for him. The order had been brief and to the point, with no room for argument. 'Report to Berchtesgaden without delay. Repeat. Without delay. At the Führer's command!' No-one kept the Führer waiting, not even an independent Austrian adventurer. Skorzeny had commandeered a plane, flown hundreds of kilometres and landed on the runway of Hitler's private airstrip at the 'wolf's lair'. Within minutes he would be once again face to face with the Führer, a prospect that daunted him. Few men looked forward to a meeting with Adolf Hitler whose moods could quickly change for little apparent reason, from back-slapping good humour to insane, uncontrollable rage. Furthermore, Skorzeny heartily disliked the sweet, sticky cakes which seemed to be Hitler's only indulgence. Young, fit and without nerves, he was also horrified at the number of pills and tranquillisers which the Führer swallowed during the course of an interview.

'Heil Hitler.' Skorzeny smartly clicked his heels and raised his arm in the Nazi salute. The tired-looking man with the pronounced stoop, lazily raised his right hand in response. The Führer looked old, much older than his years, but still had a hypnotic stare. 'I want Mussolini freed,' he began, 'it is absolutely necessary to our aims. We want him to rally the remaining Italians loyal to the Fascist cause. Get him out! Get him out at once!' Hitler then turned his back and stared out of the giant plate glass window. The audience was over.

Skorzeny left the room followed by a worried-looking Colonel of Intelligence. This officer explained the rescue plan devised by the General Staff. They secretly believed it to be doomed to failure, but they had one faint hope.

Hitler giving Skorzeny his orders – to free Mussolini at all costs

Skorzeny and the glider pilot realise the almost impossible odds against a safe landing on the tiny mountain top meadow

If the guards could be caught unawares and the hotel stormed by a party of hand-picked assault troops, there was a remote chance that Mussolini might be snatched away from his captors before they could shoot him. As Skorzeny questioned the Intelligence officer he realised the man believed the enterprise had little chance of success, but his answers came quickly enough. 'Yes', they thought there was just room to land a glider in a minute meadow behind the hotel. 'Yes'. It was a sheer drop into the valley. 'Yes'. One of Germany's best glider pilots should be used. 'No'. They could not say definitely whether or not a light aircraft would have sufficient room to take-off from the meadow. 'Yes'. It would be dashed to pieces if it went over the edge!

Skorzeny, a born leader who had the complete confidence of his men, needed all his eloquence to persuade them that this mission

had a chance. They set about their preparations for the operation muttering to themselves, and on the morning of 12 September 1943, the gliders were towed aloft into a blue sky streaked with white clouds.

'There it is! The German pilot had to shout to make himself heard above the slipstream howling past the nose of the glider. Otto Skorzeny, following the pilot's pointing finger, saw their target ahead of them: a luxury hotel perched 2,000 metres up the side of a mountain. It stood out sharply in the clear mountain air, a fairytale building hanging over the valley. A flimsy cable car was its only link with the world. All around loomed the snow-covered peaks of the Gran Sasso. Skorzeny stared in horror. 'An impregnable fortress,' he shouted. The pilot nodded. He was one of the best glider pilots in Germany, and he knew it. In the happy days before the war he had taken his glider high above the Harz mountains, and lazily spiralled round and round in the thermal currents. He remembered that he had beaten the endurance record for gliders when the Führer himself had presented him with the trophy. Hitler's words came back to him. 'Soon, we will have need of men like you.' If only he could have seen into the future. Even the Russian Front would have been preferable to this.

He stared down and his mouth began to tighten. He could feel a bead of sweat slowly crawling down the side of his nose despite the intense, numbing cold of the glider's cockpit. He tightened his grip on the control column; in a moment he was sure he would be sick. He felt, rather than heard Skorzeny say with feeling, 'I don't believe it!'

The SS man gazed at the approaching hotel. The meadow, which appeared no bigger than a pocket handkerchief, twinkled green against the dark mountain peak looming over it.

'I suppose Intelligence know what they are doing,' he shouted. There was no answer from the pilot. He was concentrating all his efforts on not being sick. He felt that Skorzeny must have nerves of steel. No-one could be expected to land an assault glider on a mere strip of grass. Suddenly, his attention was caught by a flashing light from the Junkers 52 ahead of them. 'Prepare to slip the tow-rope, sir,' he shouted.

Momentarily the tow-rope became taut as the Junkers banked to make its approach to the hotel. The glider followed it and the men inside were flung against each other. Once again on an even keel the Junkers throttled back and the tow-rope slackened. 'Slip!' shouted the pilot. The tow-rope was released and the glider rapidly began to lose speed. Quickly the noise of the wind dropped and all was quiet. The aircraft banked sharply making for its home base, its signal lamp flashing.

'They're wishing us good luck, sir!'

His sickness forgotten, the pilot was lining up the glider for landing. 'Dead ahead. Approximately two minutes to landing.'

Skorzeny turned his head and shouted, 'Check weapons.' Behind him, the tough assault troops checked the firing mechanisms of their Schmeitzers, loosened their commando knives and made sure their grenades were handy. No-one spoke. The air crackled with tension and fear. The red light went on indicating one minute to landing. They sat, grim faced, bathed in a red glow, with their knuckles shining white as they gripped the safety straps. The few seconds before the skidding crash that meant they were safely down was always the worst moment. They had ample time to consider the awful possibilities. The nose might drop and the glider turn over, breaking its back and spilling its human cargo to a horrible death. Usually, the military planners carefully selected a reasonable landing area, minimising the danger of touchdown. This time there was no choice. There was also the added danger of crashing into the mountainside, bare metres to their right, or worse still, skidding off the grass plateau out of control and crashing in the valley 2,000 metres below.

The pilot skilfully manoeuvred the glider into the correct approach path and like a great silent bird it swooped down towards the hotel. He gently eased the control column, as the bright green meadow rushed up at them.

Now! he jerked the column back and the nose went up. The glider landed belly first with a splintering crash, and they slid crabwise across the meadow. They were only metres from the hotel; it was a perfect landing.

'Out! Out!' shouted Skorzeny who was already through the door of the still skidding glider. He dashed towards the startled Italian troops who had been lounging comfortably in the sun a moment before. Confused and uncertain, they could only stare as an Italian general, who had accompanied the Germans, rushed at them shouting, 'Don't shoot, it's all right. Don't shoot.'

Panic-stricken, the guards dropped their rifles and ran. Skorzeny, followed by the leading stormtroopers three at a time, ran up the stairs to the first floor room where Mussolini was imprisoned. Taken by surprise, the Alpini officer dropped his gun and raised his hands above his head. Mussolini stepped forward to

The stormtroopers have no difficulty freeing a shaken Mussolini from the surprised Alpini soldiers

Hauptmann Gerlach, Mussolini and Skorzeny are technically too heavy a load for the Fieseler Storch to carry, particularly when the runway is so short

greet his rescuers trembling and white-faced, but could not suppress his sense of the dramatic; 'I knew my friend Adolf Hitler would not desert me.' he said. With scant patience Skorzeny hurried him down the stairs and out to the meadow. He was shocked to see that the light aircraft which was to have flown them off had damaged its undercarriage on landing. The reserve plane, a Fieseler Storch piloted by Hauptmann Gerlach one of Germany's best

pilots, landed successfully. Skorzeny pushed a protesting Mussolini into the aircraft and clambered in after him. It was a desperately tight fit. The head of the giant SS man was pressed against the cabin roof. He glanced at Mussolini. Il Duce sat white-faced – a bare hundred metres away the rock-strewn meadow ended in a sheer drop to the valley below.

Gerlach was horrified to see that Skorzeny intended to come as well. 'You too? But . . .'

'If Mussolini is killed, there will be nothing for me to do but blow out my brains. I had far better be killed with him.'

This was small comfort to Gerlach and he began to argue, but Skorzeny cut him short. 'Enough. It's the Führer's orders.'

A dozen assault troops hung on to the flimsy aircraft as Gerlach revved the engine to full power. He held up his hand. Suddenly, his hand went down and the Fieseler Storch lunged forward, gathering speed as it rushed towards the edge of the precipice. It hit a rock, slowed down then gathered speed again. Hardly airborne, the aircraft hurtled off the edge, lurched down sickeningly, then Gerlach gradually regained control and with a sigh of relief set course for the German airfield at Aquila. All three men were silent. In their hearts they knew they had just had the narrowest escape of their lives. From Aquila they flew to Vienna and then on to Berlin. Mussolini was jubilant, some of his old arrogance returning as he strutted to greet Hitler. But the cheers were for Germany's number one hero Otto Skorzeny who had pulled off yet another impossible coup.

Mussolini, his old confidence restored, is welcomed by the Führer

CHAPTER 4

The Great Locomotive Chase

Hurtling along the railway, he spotted the torn up track too late. The hand car flew off the lines and somersaulted the crew onto the muddy verge.

The Civil War in the United States in 1862 was going badly for the North. On every front the Union armies were being swept back by the victorious Confederates from the South. Led by the cream of the officers from West Point Military Academy and manned by troops fighting for their very existence, the Confederates inflicted defeat after defeat on the numerically superior and better armed Union troops. But the South's one vital weakness was that they had to rely on European countries for their arms and supplies as almost all heavy industry was situated in the North. There was also another serious weakness. They were forced to lean heavily on their railway system to bring up supplies from the deep south to the battle lines.

In Washington, military headquarters conceived a brilliant and daring plan which if successful, would strike a crippling blow to the southern railway system and reduce the flow of supplies to a mere trickle. This would relieve the pressure on the hard-pressed Union troops and, according to the more optimistic planners, shorten the war. It was felt that the sheer simplicity of the scheme was enough to ensure its success. A team of saboteurs would infiltrate into Georgia, highjack a train and then drive it north, burning down all the bridges along the route. By the time the Confederates had got their railway back into shape, the Union troops would have regrouped and steam-rollered their way south.

The General *is today one of America's most famous locomotives and a great tourist attraction*

A Union spy, James J. Andrews, was chosen to lead a commando of twenty seasoned Yankee soldiers. They posed as Southerners and travelled quite openly from the northern lines in Tennessee, south into Georgia. At dawn on 12 April 1862, they were buying tickets at Marietta station. It was exactly twelve months since the commencement of hostilities. Split into small groups, they waited on the rain-swept platform for the northbound train. They were dressed as civilians and armed with hidden revolvers and had no difficulty in mingling with the other passengers. On time, the *General*, crack locomotive of the Western and Atlantic Railway, hooted its way into the station. The Yankees dispersed along the entire length of the train, to avoid being conspicuous.

Forty-five minutes later they chugged into the station at Big Shanty. Most of the other passengers and crew made a dash through the rain to the nearby hotel, to take advantage of the routine twenty minute breakfast stop. As the other passengers scrambled to get served, the saboteurs went into action. The intelligence work had been thorough. The raiders knew the railway schedule perfectly, as well as the siting of every fuel and water supply along the route. Idly watched by a few Confederate guards who took them for railway men, they uncoupled all but three of the boxcars, and at 6.05am the *General* began to pull away from Big Shanty on its mission of destruction. Andrews was confident that they could not be followed, but he had reckoned without the stubborn determination of one man.

Inside the hotel, among the passengers clamouring to be served, was the conductor of the *General*, twenty-five year old William Fuller. Fuller was a short, stocky man who was extremely proud of being the conductor of a brand new locomotive and he took his job very seriously. Already the owners had their eyes on him and he had every hope of a successful career with the W. and A.R. He was noted for his stubborn tenacity and never would it be more in evidence than on this day.

At the first burst of steam he looked up; that sounded like his locomotive. Successive bursts convinced him that it was, and he dashed from the hotel in time to see the *General* disappearing up the track. It clattered and roared as it gathered speed, red sparks streaming from its huge, funnel-shaped smoke-stack. For a moment he stared in stunned disbelief, then he raced pell-mell after the train as it thundered north, much to the amusement of a group of onlookers on the platform. It seemed a hopeless gesture but it inspired another railwayman, Anthony Murphy, to tag along behind. Together the two men jogged on, oblivious both to the jeers of the bystanders and the pelting rain that had already soaked them to the skin.

The *General* was by now a distant smudge of black smoke, but to Fuller it was his career disappearing over the horizon. He raced on, his face grim with determination, followed by the faithful Murphy. The men on the train could hardly believe their eyes; the two 'Johnny Rebs' following them must be mad.

The two men ran alongside the single-track line for over an hour, their strength failing. They were gasping for breath and on the point of giving up when they spotted a railway section gang working on the line. They had a hand-car with them. A badly winded Fuller

William Fuller is momentarily transfixed as he sees his engine disappearing along the track

managed to gasp out his story. Some time before, the gangers had waved to the *General* as it thundered past. Come to think of it they had not recognised the engineer, but had assumed he was new to the railroad. Fuller persuaded them to manhandle the hand-car on to the rails, and with the crew pumping away for dear life, they rattled their way north at a good speed. The chase was now on in earnest. Fuller could smell blood and come what may he intended to catch up with the stolen train. Neither he nor his companions stopped to consider what they would do if they caught up with twenty armed and desperate men.

Aboard the *General* everything was running according to plan. People they had passed, farmers, railway gangers and soldiers alike, had waved to them and they had waved cheerfully back, giving a hoot on the whistle for good measure. Andrews was a careful and efficient leader. As a spy he had had to pay particular attention to detail for his life had depended on it in the past. He applied the same thinking to the present mission, and they had hardly got beyond Big Shanty when he halted the train. One of the raiders then shinned up a nearby

47

telegraph pole and cut the wires. They did this at regular intervals, so there was no likelihood of suddenly being confronted by a strong detachment of hostile Confederate troops. Andrews knew that there were no other locomotives at Big Shanty that could give chase, but as a professional spy he left nothing to chance, so, as an added precaution he ordered a section of the line to be torn up behind them.

Whenever they had to stop to load up with fuel and water, he managed to bluff his way past the often incredulous railway officials. His excuse was that the *General*, the fastest locomotive in the South, was rushing a badly needed ammunition train up to the battle front. He insisted that he be given every assistance to get it there in time for it to be of use. Some officials were suspicious, but none of them attempted to hold the train up and once it was on its way the telegraph lines were cut so that they could not communicate their suspicions to the next station. While Andrews was bluffing the railwaymen the rest of the Yankees had their revolvers handy, ready to shoot their way out of trouble if it became necessary.

Fuller, hurtling along on the hand-car, spotted the torn up track too late.

'Look out,' he cried.

The hand car flew off the lines and somersaulted the crew on to the muddy verge. Bruised and bespattered with mud they righted the hand-car and manhandled it back on to the rails. Then they were off again, by now a bunch of very angry and determined men. They realised that they were chasing 'Damned Yankees' and not just ordinary train thieves. The sweat streamed off them as they put all their energy into their pumping. Then the situation changed quite dramatically. Union Intelligence had overlooked an old shunting engine when they had planned the mission. It was used by an ironworks to carry the ore to the main line. This was Fuller's big chance. Quickly it was shunted to the main line, and accompanied by a number of armed Confederate soldiers, he steamed after the *General*. Fuller and Murphy piled wood into the little *Yonah*'s fire box, and with her smoke-stack red-hot, the old shunting locomotive swayed and clattered northwards. Never before had she reached such

Fuller and his friends are angered rather than deterred by the methods used by the Yankees to try and make them give up the chase

speeds, and the men crammed together on the footplate were flung from side to side as she swayed perilously on.

At Kingston station they screeched to a halt in a shower of sparks; their way was blocked by a line of freight cars. Fuller was dismayed to learn that the *General* had gone through some

time before. The Yankees were still a long way ahead. Fuller had guessed at the purpose of the raid, and was more than ever determined to catch up with the raiders. Not for one moment did this tenacious little man think of giving up the chase. He was determined to catch up with the Yankees and foil their plans. He ran ahead to the freight locomotive, the *W.R. Smith*, a fine powerful engine, and clambered aboard, followed closely by his private army. The southerners got up steam while the local railwaymen unhooked the freight cars, and within minutes they were chugging out of Kingston, rapidly gathering speed. The excite-

ment mounted in the cab of the locomotive. They were in hot pursuit and their quarry within striking distance and in the heat of the moment someone gave a piercing blast on the train whistle.

Up ahead, Andrews heard the plaintive shriek of the whistle and knew that somehow, someone had taken up the chase and that it could only be a matter of time before their pursuers caught up with them. The *General* braked to a halt and some of the raiders, led by Andrews, jumped off the locomotive and frantically tore at the rails with heavy crowbars. They worked feverishly until they had one section loose. They rolled it down an embankment then ran back and jumped aboard the *General*. That would put a stop to any further pursuit. The laughing Yankees were now quite confident that they would succeed in their mission. Soon now they would be coming up to the bridges they had been detailed to burn down.

Fuller was taking no chances. He hung on to the *W. R. Smith*'s cowcatcher at the front of the train, on the watch for damaged lines, and he was in plenty of time to warn the engineer when they came up to the derailed track. The locomotive shuddered to a halt metres from disaster. The plucky little conductor, refusing to be beaten, jumped to the ground and began running again. But Fuller's luck held. Fifteen minutes later he sighted a south-bound freight train, the *Texas*, and ran towards it down the track frantically waving his arms. The startled engineer listened to Fuller, but it took time to convince him and the conductor that the story was true. But finally the *Texas* was reversing up the line towards the next station. Here the

The Yankees attempt once again to derail their pursuers but Fuller is prepared for them this time and averts disaster

freight cars were slipped and the locomotive, still in reverse, took up the headlong chase. The gap between the locomotives was slowly but surely being narrowed, the vengeful shriek of the *Texas's* whistle becoming louder and louder. At Dalton Fuller managed to telegraph a warning message to the Confederate troops ahead before the Yankees could cut the wires.

No-one was laughing aboard the *General* now. They could hardly believe that it was possible for anyone to have kept up the chase, yet they could hear the sound of the whistle behind them getting louder. Desperate by this time, Andrews stopped the train, and he and his men tore madly at the track behind them, but their panic-stricken efforts were to no avail. The *Texas* was now in sight and a hail of bullets sent the raiders scurrying back to their locomotive.

Slowly, Fuller's engine bore down on the *General*. The two locomotives roared through the driving rain, past farms and over streams and rivers, the raiders so hotly pursued that they were unable to destroy the bridges. They had failed in their mission, and the only thought in their minds now was to escape at all costs. They were well aware that to be captured in civilian clothes would mean a firing squad. From the rear boxcar some of the Yankees hurled heavy wooden sleepers on to the line in an effort to delay the *Texas*. This slowed the locomotive to a walking pace. Fuller, once again to the fore, went ahead to clear the track. Twice the raiders released boxcars, sending them hurtling wildly down gradients head-on towards the *Texas*. Both times the Confederate engineer managed to brake quickly, put the locomotive into reverse and take up the boxcars while moving in the same direction. The *Texas* then pushed the boxcars to the next station; they were slipped, and the chase went on.

Shortly before 11.0 am the *General* came to

Fuller, displaying great courage, once more saves the day as he releases the blazing box car

the long covered railway bridge across the Chickamanga Creek. Andrews knew that this was his last chance to achieve at least part of his mission. He ordered the engineer to stop the *General* in the centre of the wooden bridge. He and his men slipped the remaining boxcar and despite its wet condition managed to set it ablaze. Soon the flames were licking up the sides of the covered bridge and the raiders made off, confident that at last they had avoided their relentless pursuers.

A few minutes later, Fuller stared out of the cab of the *Texas* and was horrified to see the Chickamanga bridge a mass of flames. As they approached Fuller realised that the main part of the fire was centred round the boxcar and the wooden canopy overhead, while luckily the bridge itself was only just beginning to catch fire. He slowed the *Texas* down and chugged on

to the bridge attempting to push the blazing boxcar ahead of it, but the Union raiders had wedged a tie under the wheels, jamming it fast. Fuller jumped down and made his way across the bridge to the burning car. Enveloped in flames, his clothes smouldering, he struggled to loosen the tie. At last he managed to free it, then he ran across the bridge and flung himself into the shallow creek. Meanwhile the locomotive pushed the blazing box car across the bridge and shunted it into a nearby siding where it burnt itself out.

Shortly after, the men in the *Texas* sighted the *General*, but coming towards them. The Yankees had run out of fuel and had set the *General* in reverse and abandoned her. As she rolled towards them, going far too slowly to cause any damage, Fuller smiled for the first time since the highjacking. He had won.

Andrews and his men scattered, taking to the hills. Separately, they attempted to make it back to the Union lines, but the telegraph message from Dalton had alerted the Confederates and one by one the raiders were picked up. The chase had lasted for nearly five hours, covering a distance of 139 kilometres. The tenacious Fuller, modest in victory, is reported to have said: 'You cannot blame them for running out of fuel.'

CHAPTER 5

Shark Encounter

They floated on the surface in a terribly vulnerable position, their legs a natural target for the killers below.

For several weeks, Jacques Cousteau and his team had been diving in the shark-infested waters round the Cape Verde Islands off the coast of Africa in the North Atlantic. Their little ship, the *Elie Monnier*, was anchored close to an exposed coral reef hit by the long Atlantic rollers. Walls of spray were sent high into the air. It was a beautiful sunny day, just made for diving. The water was crystal clear and ideal for filming.

Time and again, day in, day out, the Cousteau team had been making dive after dive filming various aspects of the marine life that teemed round the reefs. As soon as the *Elie Monnier* had anchored anywhere it had been surrounded by sharks of every species, and the divers always took precautionary measures when they were under water. One day, towards the beginning of the expedition, Cousteau himself was making a camera dive, filming a sequence on trigger fish. His companion, Dumas, with his harpoon gun at the ready, was acting as his bodyguard slowly circling above him as he filmed. Cousteau looked up to see Dumas frantically waving to him. He was struck with cold terror:

a giant fish had suddenly appeared out of the gloom 12 metres away and was lazily swimming towards them. It was a shark at least 7 metres long from its pointed snout to the tip of its tail. It was lead-white in colour and belonged to a species of confirmed man-eaters.

Instinctively, the two startled men closed together; two puny naked creatures faced by a dreadful killer of the deep, one snap of whose fearful jaws could easily take off a leg.

'In that moment,' Cousteau writes, 'I thought that at least he would have a belly-ache on our cylinder lungs.' It was obvious to the two men that the monster had not seen them yet, but it would only be seconds before it did. However, if they swam off with a flurry it would see them at once, and they knew that they had no chance of out-swimming it. While they hesitated, the shark saw them. To their amazement, the shark, in sheer fright, sent out a cloud of excrement and swam off at incredible speed.

After this encounter, Cousteau and his team became more and more confident about meeting sharks. They went out of their way to seek them out. Confident in their own superiority, they met all varieties head-on. The sharks, whether large or small, harmless or known man-eaters, in every instance turned tail and swam away. As time went on, they reached the conclusion that all sharks were cowards. This made them over-confident and led to foolish negligence. They abandoned the bodyguard system and other safety measures. Once, during the filming of a shark sequence, three nurse sharks were discovered asleep in a cave. The film called for active sharks so two of the younger members of the team swam into the cave and pulled their tails to waken them. Obligingly, the sharks shot out and were filmed as they swam off.

As it was such good weather, Cousteau decided to head for the open sea and try for some deep-sea filming. Soon the *Elie Monnier*

Cousteau and Dumas, terrified by the shark, are amazed to find that the giant creature is even more frightened of them

had weighed anchor, left the reef, and was cutting her way through the Atlantic swell, out of sight of the African coast. Suddenly there was a shout from the deck. 'Whales!'

A school of bottlenosed whales, sluggishly surfacing in the clear water, surrounded them. Dumas ran to the harpoon platform at the bow while Cousteau loaded a film magazine into the underwater camera. A small bottlenose surfaced 4 metres from Dumas. He hurled the harpoon, the shaft went in cleanly behind the pectoral fin and the whale sounded, plummeting vertically towards the sea-bed.

Cousteau and Dumas entered the water to follow the harpoon line down to the stricken whale; Dumas was to pass a noose over the whale's tail while Cousteau filmed. 5 metres down the line they sighted a two and a half metre shark. It was light grey and sleek, and was a species they had never seen before. It was swimming parallel to the divers with its little eyes fixed unblinkingly on the two men. Its deadly, streamlined shape appeared to glide through the water with hardly a movement of its powerful tail. Confidently, the swimmers made towards it, fully expecting it to go from them as the others had done. But the shark turned to face them. It was now within 3 metres of them and they could see clearly the tiny black and white, vertically striped pilot fish, which appeared glued to the shark's snout, while other pilot fish swam above its back. The shark, with its entourage, glided past the divers and began to circle them. Still the two men had no sense of danger. Boldly Dumas swam up to the grey beast and grasped its tail; the shark made no hostile move but glided swiftly away, its small beady eyes gazing steadily at the two men. Cousteau continued filming and the shark continued to circle them.

Unwittingly they had allowed themselves to be gradually drawn down to a depth of about 20 metres. Dumas pointed: climbing towards them out of the depths came two more sharks, steel-blue savage-looking brutes, all of 5 metres long. Inconsequentially, the divers noticed that the sharks had no accompanying pilot fish. They levelled out just below the swimmers, who at last had begun to sense danger. The grey shark continued its slow clock-wise circuit, but the circle was becoming ever smaller; slowly

but surely it was closing in on the two men. The divers revolved inside the circle and desperately tried to watch the grey and at the same time keep an eye on the blue pair circling below them. Trapped between the two, they could neither make for the surface nor go down.

Dumas harpooning a small, bottlenosed whale. Inset: Jacques Cousteau

By now the two men were badly scared. They fought to recall every piece of advice they had ever been given for frightening off sharks. They waved their arms and shouted until they were hoarse. The grey showed no reaction but calmly continued its leisurely circuit. A helmet-diver had once told Cousteau that sharks ran from 'a flood of bubbles', so when the grey reached its nearest point to them, which was now desperately close, the two men released a flood of air. Two streams of bubbles flowed out towards the shark. It took no notice but swam straight through them. Luckily, Cousteau had strapped a tablet of cupric acetate to his ankle before entering the water. This well-tried shark repellent was used by the Air Force and had never been known to fail. When the grey shark scented the chemical it would make off, or at least move away sufficiently to allow them to reach the surface and safety. But the unnatural brute swam through the copper-stained water without a qualm, unhurriedly closing in on the two men.

The circle was now very small indeed, and on the shark's next circuit a horrifying thing happened. When it had reached its nearest point when the divers could almost touch it, the tiny pilot fish wriggled away from the grey's snout and swam to Dumas, fluttering in front of his mask. Desperately, he shook his head and waved his arms violently, but the pilot fish happily moved with the mask. For a moment Cousteau's attention was diverted by the playful antics of the little striped fish, then he saw Dumas snatch out his belt knife. He looked round and saw the grey shark, which had swum some distance off, turn, and come at them like an express train. He turned to meet it head-on, but armed as they were, with only a knife and camera, the odds were hopelessly stacked against the two men. Instinctively, Cousteau continued to film the shark as it flashed towards him. The dreadful jaws grew larger until they filled the whole of the view-finder. The grey was about to strike, when Cousteau, with all his force, crashed the heavy

Instinctively, Cousteau continues to film the shark as it flashes towards him. The camera then becomes a life-saver as Cousteau uses it as a weapon to ward off the beast

camera down on its snout. He felt the huge body rush past him, then once more the shark was back in position slowly circling the divers, 3 metres away.

Now the two blue sharks swam up to join the grey. The odds were impossible; it was only a question of time before they closed in for the kill. If the two men were to survive they had to do something quickly. Their best chance lay in making a dash for the surface and attracting the attention of the men aboard the *Elie Monnier*.

The three sharks band together to attack the two men

Keeping close together they swam rapidly upwards towards the light. Their heads broke the surface and they saw the *Elie Monnier* less than 270 metres away. They waved and shouted, but there was no reply from the ship.

They floated on the surface in a terribly vulnerable position, their legs a natural target for the killers below. Cousteau looked down: the three sharks were coming at them in a concerted attack. The men dived to meet them and immediately the sharks took up their circling manoeuvre, hesitating to attack at two fathoms. Most recorded attacks by sharks have been against swimmers, whose flashing legs, breaking up the light close to the surface, act as a lure to the man-eaters. Cousteau and Dumas realised that their only hope of escape was to make for the ship, but how could they pinpoint its position at that depth? They could only take it in turns to swim to the surface, wave and shout and note the *Elie Monnier*'s position, then dive again and face the sharks. Meanwhile, the

other man would keep watch below, with his knees up to his chin acting on the theory that sharks usually attacked legs.

Gradually by these means they managed to draw near to the ship, but it was a tediously slow process, and often they became confused and found themselves moving away from the *Elie Monnier*. At one point, when Dumas was swimming up to the surface, one of the blue sharks eluded Cousteau and made for Dumas's feet. Cousteau shouted a warning and his companion resolutely turned to face the attack. The blue shark broke away and rejoined the circle. For half-an-hour the three sharks played this cat and mouse game with the two swimmers until they were near the point of exhaustion, and a deadly cold was beginning to creep over their bodies. Still there was no sign that they had been spotted by the *Elie Monnier*. They were aware that at any moment their oxygen supply would run out, and leave them only five minutes of air in their emergency bottles. It was a daunting prospect. They would have to abandon their mouth-pieces and holding their breath rely on mask dives. In their weakened condition they would not be able to keep this up for long. Sooner or later it meant a fearful death, when the sharks closed in for the final attack.

The sharks increased their speed almost as if they sensed the men's position. Back to back the divers strove to watch all three of the man-eaters, but it was becoming more and more difficult. Cousteau and Dumas had all but given themselves up for lost, when without any apparent reason the three sharks turned and disappeared into the depths below. The two men could hardly believe their eyes. What new devilry was this? Then a shadow fell across them – it was the hull of the ship's launch. Their signals had been spotted from the *Elie Monnier* at some time during their surface dashes and the launch which set out to locate their bubbles had frightened away the sharks.

The two men flopped gratefully into the boat, weak and badly shaken but very much the wiser.

'The better acquainted we become with sharks,' Cousteau was later to write, 'the less we know them, and one can never tell what a shark is going to do.'

CHAPTER 6

Trek across the Outback

*One dreadful morning
they woke up to find that the
natives had disappeared in the night.
They were now forced to fend
for themselves.*

'God speed and bless you.'

At these words, spoken by the Mayor of Melbourne, the expedition moved off to the cheers of the holiday crowd gathered in the Royal Park. The year was 1860, and Robert O'Hara Burke and his party were setting off in an attempt to cross the continent from south to north. At this time Melbourne was by far the most important town in Australia. It had mushroomed from a small pastoral settlement with bewildering suddenness. Ten years earlier it had been a little-known outpost of New South Wales, cut off from the rest of Australia, without road, rail or telegraphic links with the remainder of the continent. Then in 1850 the Queen had agreed to a new colony being set up south of the Murray River which would be named after her, Victoria. The following year gold was discovered near Ballarat.

Gold fever swept the new colony. Men gave up safe jobs to take their chance prospecting at the diggings. Prices rocketed and gold-hungry adventurers flocked into Melbourne. Overnight a poorly-paid clerk could become a rich man. The 'Welcome Stranger' nugget was found only six centimetres below the surface; weighing 57 grams it was worth £9,534. The gold rush brought with it more than its share of evils; thieving and killing, drunkenness and general lawlessness. This was the heyday of the notorious bushrangers who roamed the outback and waylaid the coaches bringing the newly-won gold to be banked in Melbourne. But the lawlessness of the gold-rush quickly subsided when the alluvial gold supply was

W. J. Wills   Captain Dana.   R. O. Burke.
(figure holding surveying instrument).

exhausted. There was still plenty of gold but now it had to be mined with machinery, and the big mining company replaced the individual prospector. Life gradually returned to normal but Melbourne had gained enormously from its brief influx of wealth. It was no longer cut off

Dr. Becker.   Mr. Landells   Ambulance for carrying
(who had charge of the camels).   the sick.

*A contemporary engraving of the Burke and Wills
expedition moving off from Melbourne*

from the rest of Australia for a railway had been constructed in the late fifties, and soon after it was linked to Adelaide and Sydney by telegraph. A young American named Cobb, introduced mammoth coaches. They were drawn by twenty-two horses and each coach was capable of carrying nearly a hundred passengers.

By 1860 Melbourne was a flourishing state capital. Its streets were lit by gas and it boasted

63

a Parliament House, public library, university, a string of commercial banks and a theatre that could seat 4,000. A racecourse had been laid out and the Melbourne Cup was run for the first time. It also had learned societies, and one of these, the Philosophical Institute of Victoria and later, having been granted a Royal Charter, known as the Royal Society, turned its attention to the exploration of the Australian interior.

Inland from the coast the territory was virtually unexplored. The continent itself, so old, so untouched, was like nowhere else on earth. There were no traces of former civilisations, for there had never been any. The natives of Australia, the naked Aborigines, were the most primitive people in the world who still lived in the Stone Age. Caught in an endless dream, they built no villages, planted no crops, domesticated no animals. They were truly nomadic. They wandered through the bush in small groups hunting and foraging for roots and berries. The only relief from their eternal fight for survival was the occasional tribal ceremonies, when they daubed themselves with white clay and performed rituals as old as time. The land itself was bleak and uninviting and the leaves of the trees were grey rather than green.

It was known that from the time of the earliest settlers the further one probed inland, the hotter and drier it became. As the nineteenth century advanced, adventurous explorers such as Charles Sturt and Gregory began to penetrate the wilderness. By 1846 Sturt had reached the twenty-fifth latitude. North of that the map was a complete blank, totally unknown territory. Many people believed that an inland sea, another Mediterranean, lay somewhere at the centre of the continent. In 1860 the question still remained; could the continent be crossed from south to north? It was not curiosity alone that prompted people to pose the question. A telegraph line from the south to the northern coast, linking up with the cable that already extended through India to south-

Many old customs and ceremonies prevail amongst the 20,000 full-blooded Aborigines still living in Australia

east Asia would cut the existing four-month communication gap with London down to a few hours. There was also the tempting possibility of opening up trade routes to China and south-east Asia.

The Royal Society at one of their meetings decided to investigate the possibility of a trans-continental expedition, and an exploration committee was set up. The proposed Victorian Exploration Expedition appealed to the colony's civic pride, and a prosperous provision merchant, Ambrose Kyte, offered to put up £1,000, provided that a further £2,000 could be raised by public subscription within one year. It was. The Victoria Government, prompted to action, voted a further £6,000 towards the expenses of the expedition. With more than £9,000 at their disposal the exploration committee could fit out the enterprise on a lavish scale.

An advertisement in the Melbourne press for an expedition leader brought fourteen replies. A police superintendent from the Castlemaine District was chosen from these applicants by ten votes to five. Robert Burke was a surprising choice, and in the light of subsequent events, an unwise one. Born in Ireland, he came from a military and land-owning family in County Galway. At an early age he served with an Austrian cavalry regiment. Later he enlisted in the Irish Constabulary and from there joined the Victoria police, in which he quickly rose to the important position of superintendent.

He was still unmarried and at 39 had gained the reputation of being mildly eccentric and very reckless. One contemporary wrote of him: 'He was a careless daredevil sort of Irishman of very ordinary physique.' Another wrote: 'He was kind and generous to a fault but if anything happened out of the common routine he became confused, then excited, till finally he would lose control of his better judgement.' Yet another wrote: 'He was a wild eccentric daredevil. Either he did not realise danger or his mind was unhinged to the extent that he revelled in it.' But the most damning comment was: 'He was the worst bushman I ever met.' Surely this should have disqualified him from leading an expedition that called for the qualities of patience, tact, understanding and dogged determination.

George James Landells, a reputed expert with camels, was chosen as Burke's second-in-command, and he was sent immediately to India to purchase twenty-seven of the beasts, as it was believed that much of the route would be through desert and semi-desert. Among the other members of the expedition was a serious young Englishman named William John Wills, who was taken along as surveyor. Despite their difference in age and temperament, Wills had a precise, tidy mind, and the two men struck up an immediate friendship which was to last right up to the very end.

The expedition straggled out of the Royal Park in two parallel columns because the horses were terrified of the camels and refused to go near them. Burke took up his position in the centre, riding his horse Billy. His letter of instruction from the committee was vague and misleading. It stipulated that Cooper's Creek, a watercourse in the desert over 1,280 kilometres north of Melbourne, should be, 'the basis of your operations.' Apart from that he was virtually given a free hand to travel in whatever direction he thought appropriate. This rather slipshod attitude was reflected throughout the whole of the expedition.

From the outset there was bad blood between Burke and Landells, which came to a head at Menindie, when Landells resigned and made his way back to Melbourne. His resignation underlined the fact that the expedition had split itself into two camps. The older members were dissatisfied with Burke's slapdash yet curiously autocratic leadership, while the younger ones gave him their whole-hearted support. Wills was promoted to second-in-command and on 19 October, an advance party of eight men marched out of Menindie heading north. Their objective, Cooper's Creek, was 640 kilometres away across unexplored ground that was probably waterless. Burke completely ignored the advice given to him by the settlers at Menindie, who claimed that it was madness to travel into the desert during the hot season. But there was one good reason for pressing on. Stuart, an experienced explorer, who had already led a number of successful sorties into the outback, was getting together an expedition to cross the continent from Adelaide. There was a prize of several thousand pounds if he

Robert Burke

succeeded. The Melbourne *Punch* printed a poem, entitled, 'The Great Australian Exploration Race'.

> *'A race! A race! so great a one*
> *The world ne'er saw before;*
> *A race! A race! across the land*
> *From south to northern shore.*
>
> *The horseman hails from Adelaide*
> *The camel rider's ours*
> *Now let the steed maintain his speed*
> *Against the camel's powers.'*

They struck out into the wilderness, hoping to make 32 kilometres a day and therefore Cooper's Creek in under a month. For days travelling at a good pace they marched over plains carpeted with early spring flowers, magenta-coloured wild hops and everlasting daisies. A party of eight had no reason to be afraid of the Aborigines who appeared from time to time, staring at them open-mouthed and scuttling off when the explorers tried to make

John King

William Wills

friendly overtures. The natives were treated with the utmost suspicion and were regarded as a potential danger until the later stages of the expedition. At every camp site the explorers cut the letter 'B' and a Roman numeral into a tree, to guide the rear party following in their wake with the bulk of the stores.

They were forced to wear goggles and veils as a protection against the choking dust and the flies. These they found particularly irksome in

the scorching heat of the desert. On 11 November, 23 days out of Menindie, they arrived at Cooper's Creek. The creek, had huge waterholes, and was wooded with eucalyptus. It was a welcome sight and they hastened to set up camp. However, later a plague of rats drove them to move camp some kilometres downstream. It made an ideal depot. Birds of every kind flitted among the trees and the creek itself was alive with fish and fresh-water mussels. It seemed like Paradise.

The main party had not arrived by mid-December, so Burke, impatient to be off, decided to make a dash for the Gulf of Carpentaria with a party of four: himself, Wills, Gray and King. The depot party were Brahe, the foreman, Patton, McDonough and a Pathan, Dost Mahomet. Burke and his companions, with the six best camels, started out for the Gulf. Before he left he gave Brahe careful instructions. Burke had no intention of waiting for a south-bound ship when they reached the north coast. They would retrace their steps

overland and could be expected back at Cooper's Creek within a maximum of three months. Should they fail to turn up within this period, Brahe was to hang on for as long as his stores lasted, and then as a last resort make for Menindie. But Burke failed to give Brahe any written instructions, which caused considerable controversy at a later date.

In the early dawn on Sunday, 16 December, the camels were packed and they set off. They were doing precisely what they had been advised not to do, travel in mid-summer. They had with them for provisions 45 kilos of dried horse flesh, 152 kilos of flour, 23 kilos of oatmeal, 45 kilos of bacon, 14 kilos of biscuits, 23 kilos of sugar, 5 kilos of tea and 2 kilos of salt. They hoped these stores would last them for three months. They carried guns and ammunition, hoping to shoot game along the way, but oddly enough they did not take any tents with them. None of them had any knowledge of

medicine and the original expedition doctor had resigned with Landells and stayed on at Menindie, so if any of them became ill they would have to fend for themselves as best they could.

Of the four of them, only Gray who was in his forties, was in any way a bushman. The others had gained what little experience they had on the trip out from Melbourne. Now ahead of them lay 1,200 kilometres of unexplored territory, containing unknown hazards that could well call for the experience of a seasoned explorer. The youngest of the four, King, was only 22 years of age, but he was a strong, willing man and a good person to have in a tight corner. Burke was the unquestioned leader, the others accepting his decisions even when they doubted his judgement. With Wills acting as navigator they began the long walk to

*The expedition moving slowly across many kilometres
of desolate countryside*

the Gulf of Carpentaria. The animals were ridden only at really critical moments.

Travelling north they marched from one waterhole to the next. They were forced to make lengthy detours by impassable swamps and rocky outcrops. They were particularly troubled by sandstorms, which sometimes blew for days on end, covering everything with a layer of fine red sand. By Boxing Day they had crossed Sturt's stony desert and in early January they were travelling in more fertile country, moving towards the Selwyn Range. This 300 metre high range, made up of rugged quartz, was crossed by 20 January and they

entered the tropics, having covered 800 kilometres of their journey. They were overtaken by the rainy season with 272 kilometres still to go. Day after day warm rain poured down, which soaked them to the skin as they floundered about in the mud. They travelled by moonlight, to avoid the humid heat of the day, following the Cloncurry River to its confluence with the Flinders River, one of whose tributaries, the Byno, led down to the sea. When they were 48 kilometres away from the sea

Burke decided it was impossible to take the camels any further, as they were totally unused to the boggy ground. They made camp, and carved the inevitable number on a nearby tree. It had now reached CXIX. Leaving Gray and King in charge of the camels, Burke and Wills set out next day to try to reach the coast. They had rations for only three days. They struggled through the heavy rain but were finally halted by an inpenetrable mangrove swamp, so, with rations running low they had to return to their camp without having sighted the sea.

Back in camp the four men reviewed the situation. They had taken 57 days on the outward journey from Cooper's Creek, and despite a frugal daily ration they had eaten more than two thirds of their provisions. The remaining rations, 38 kilos of flour, just over a kilo of pork, 11 kilos of dried meat, 5 kilos of biscuits and 5 kilos of rice, would last them for just a month, if they were careful. It was just half as much as they would need for the return to the depot. Burke was not overconcerned. He knew that the rations could be supplemented by portulaca, a succulent plant which they ate boiled, and such birds as they could shoot, although this had not proved very successful as a source of food on the way out. They also still had the camels if the worst came to the worst. On the journey north they had managed between 19 and 24 kilometres a day, and Burke could see no reason why they should not repeat this performance on the return to Cooper's Creek. Everything appeared to be in their favour; the animals were carrying lighter loads and they now knew the way. All of them were reasonably fit, apart from Gray who complained of headaches, which Burke brushed aside as malingering. Ideally, both they and the animals would have benefited from a few weeks' rest, but the shortage of food made any delay impossible. The basic daily ration was reduced to 12 sticks of dried meat and 113gms of flour for each man. They began the homeward journey after only one day's rest.

The rain continued to beat down with miserable persistence, and Burke, whose diary was meagre at the best of times, now made no notes at all. Even Wills, whose journal on the outward march was precise and informative, now became slack, and his four to five hundred

Route of Burke and Wills

0   500m
0   300km

words a day dwindled to short comments. He contented himself with noting down dates and the names of camps. His growing weariness can be measured by the increasing scrappiness of his entries. In fact, the four men were far more tired than they realised and dragging themselves and the animals through the clinging mud called for a supreme effort. They were exhausted at the end of a day and would flop down to sleep on the wet ground, convinced now that they should have brought the tents.

They struggled on for a week, their stamina

being rapidly sapped by the muddy conditions they had to endure. At the end of this time Wills wrote in his diary: 'Between four and five o'clock a heavy thunderstorm broke over us, having given very little warning of its approach. There had been lightning and thunder towards the south-east and south ever since noon yesterday. The rain was incessant and very heavy for an hour and a half, which made the ground so boggy that the animals could scarcely walk over it. We nevertheless, started at 6.50am, and after floundering along for half-an-hour, halted for breakfast. We then moved on again, but found that the travelling was too heavy for the camels, so we camped for the remainder of the day. In the afternoon the sky cleared a little, and the sun soon dried the ground, considering. Shot a pheasant, and much disappointed at finding him all feather and claws.'

Gray's headaches continued and King too began to complain of pains in his arms and legs; the appalling conditions were beginning to take their toll. Wills notes in his diary: 'The evening (23 February) was most oppressively hot and sultry, so much so that the slightest exertion made one feel as if he were in state of suffocation.' They found it impossible to make anywhere near 19 kilometres a day. The ration was barely adequate and once, following the example of the Aborigines, they tried eating a large snake which they had killed. This proved to be a mistake. Burke complained of giddiness almost immediately after eating it and for two miserable days he dragged himself along suffering from acute dysentery.

After three weeks they had covered only 160 kilometres, but as they neared the desert the prospect of travelling in dry conditions raised their spirits. Only Gray failed to respond. He was by now complaining continuously about

Following the eating habits of the Aborigines the explorers kill a snake for food

his health, yet Burke and the others still believed he was 'gammoning', and he received no special treatment. When he was caught stealing food Burke gave him a good thrashing.

Each day they covered less ground and after forty days they were still only halfway to the depot. However, the Selwyn Range was behind them and they were confident of making better time in the bracing desert air of the centre of the country. Unfortunately, this did not prove to be the case for persistent rain continued to hold them back, and they began to discard all but the

most essential equipment. In case they ever returned they hung it from trees. It marked their passage, mute evidence of their growing weakness and uncertainty. They killed all but two of the camels for food, and on 10 April Wills wrote in his diary: 'Remained at Camp LIIR all day to cut up and jerk the meat of the horse Billy, who was so reduced and knocked up through want of food, that there appeared to be little chance of his reaching the other side of the desert; and as we were running short of food of every description ourselves, we thought it best to secure his flesh at once.' But they were by now very feeble and only able to carry a fraction of the carcass of any animal they slaughtered.

Gray was, by this time, so weak and ill that he could no longer ride by himself and had to be strapped to a camel, yet the others continued to think that he was not as ill as he made out. But Gray was not 'gammoning', as Wills' entry for 17 April shows. 'This morning about sunrise, Gray died. He had not spoken a word distinctly since his first attack, which was just as we were about to start.'

The remaining three were now so frail that it took them a whole day to dig a grave one metre deep in which to bury him. Gray's death had a profound effect on the morale of the others. Burke in particular was prepared to take any risks to shorten the time reaching the depot. The next day, before setting out, they abandoned all their remaining equipment; but nothing would persuade Wills to leave his precious note books, which contained the only record of their achievements.

They pushed painfully on, now less than 112 kilometres from Cooper's Creek. They were stark, bearded figures covered only in tattered rags with their boots worn down to the uppers. They spent the bitterly cold nights without covering, huddled round a fire. As they neared Cooper's Creek a party of natives appeared who made friendly overtures to the ragged white men and followed them at a distance until they camped. On 19 April Wills wrote: 'Camped again without water on the sandy bed of the creek, having been followed by a lot of natives who were desirous of our company. The night was very cold.'

The end of the next day's march brought

them within 48 kilometres of the depot. Elated, they divided up the remaining food and made a good meal. At first light they were determined to start a march that would take them to Cooper's Creek in a day. When they turned in that night they had visions of the reception they would receive when they surprised the depot party the following evening. In the early dawn they moved off. They marched on and on, long past the normal point of collapse. Doggedly they put one foot in front of the other, driven on by the thoughts of food and companionship waiting for them a few short kilometres ahead.

As they neared the site of the depot they broke into a feeble jog.

'Coo-ee, Coo-ee'. Their bushman's call echoed through the silent trees. 'Coo-ee! Coo-ee!'

'Brahe, Patton, McDonough!' There was no answer. Inside the wooden stockade they found all the signs of a recent departure. The ground was littered with bits of equipment, and there were fresh traces of horse and cattle dung. Had they just moved camp to further up the creek? They caught sight of a fresh blaze on one of the trees. It read: 'Dig 3 feet (a metre) north-west. 21 April 1861'. Their faces were haggard with despair as they paced out the distance and began to dig. Half a metre down they unearthed a box containing rations and a letter – a letter bearing that day's date.

'Depot Cooper's Creek, 21 April 1861.

The depot party of the VEE (Victorian Exploring Expedition) leaves camp today to return to the Darling. I intend to go south-east from Camp LX to get into our old track near Bullow. Two of my companions and myself are quite well: the third, Patton, has been unable to walk for the last eighteen days, as his leg was severely hurt when thrown by one of the horses. No person has been up here from the Darling.

We have six camels and twelve horses in good working condition.

William Brahe

The three exhausted survivors arrive at Cooper's Creek, only to find that they have missed the depot party by a few hours

The three men read the letter in shocked silence. Gradually they saw the tragic irony of the situation. They had marched 2,430 kilometres in four months, under harrowing conditions, and had missed the depot party by a few hours. It was no wonder that Burke collapsed in despair, too far gone to attempt to catch up the depot party who were probably camping no more than 32 kilometres away.

Why had Brahe gone? Why had he abandoned them? His orders had been explicit; he was to wait until his stores ran out. Burke blustered that he would have Brahe and his men punished when he returned to Melbourne, but there was a hollow ring to his threats. In the back of each of their minds lurked the fearful conviction that none of them were ever likely to see Melbourne again.

On 23 April, after listlessly hanging about the camp for two days, they moved off down the south bank of Cooper's Creek. They first buried a message under the same tree in case a search party should be sent to find them. They took the opposite direction from Brahe and his party, intending to travel down the creek for about 64 kilometres and then cut off across the desert to a police post at Mount Hopeless, some 240 kilometres away. From there they would be able to continue through settled districts to Adelaide. The explorer Gregory had managed the same journey in about a week.

Their attitude to the Aborigines changed considerably over the next few days. A fishing party gave them 5 kilos of fresh fish in exchange for some matches and a few scraps of leather. The next day they arrived with another present of fish, causing Wills to write, rather patronisingly: 'They are by far the most well-behaved blacks we have seen on Cooper's Creek.' As they continued to follow the creek at a leisurely pace, both men and animals gained in strength. This brought with it a corresponding rise in spirits. 'The comparative rest,' wrote Wills, 'and the change in diet have worked wonders; the leg-tied feeling has now completely gone, and I believe in less than a week we shall be fit to undergo any fatigue whatsoever.'

When everything appeared to be going well, disaster struck. Landa, one of the two camels, stumbled into a quicksand and had to be shot.

The three white men rely totally on the kindness of the Aborigines for their survival

They cut off what meat they could then pressed on, but the incident did much to sap their new-found confidence. Left with only one camel they explored the channels of the creek leading in the direction of Mount Hopeless, but each one petered out leaving them faced with bleak desert.

Wills wrote: 'This dreary prospect offered no inducement to proceed.' He was very

despondent. 'The present state of things is not calculated to raise our spirits much. The rations are rapidly diminishing: our clothes, especially the boots, are all going to pieces, and we have not the materials for repairing them properly. The camel is completely done up, and can scarcely get along, although he has the best of feed and is resting half the time. I suppose this will end in our having to live like the blacks for a few months.' They had accepted the possi-bility that they would have to sit tight on the creek until a rescue party turned up. But their continuing survival very much depended on receiving help from the Aborigines. Without it they would never be able to survive.

The Aborigines had taken to the strange white men who seemed to wander about aimlessly looking for nothing in particular, and were ready to welcome them into their tribe. They gave them food and pitchery, a drug made by roasting the stems of a native shrub. 'After chewing it for few minutes,' said King, 'I felt quite happy and perfectly indifferent about my position,' They made one last desperate effort to break away from the creek, but after travelling 72 kilometres without finding water they reluctantly had to turn back. It was brought home to them that they could not leave the creek, and must somehow, with the help of the natives, stay alive until they were rescued.

One dreadful morning they woke up to find that the natives had disappeared in the night. They were now forced to fend for themselves. It was only then that they fully realised just how much they had come to depend on the Aborigines for help. By the third week in June the three men were nearly spent. Wills was failing rapidly and insisted that the only hope was for the two others to go in search of the natives. They could leave him in a hut with enough food within reach to last him until their return. Burke and King painfully set out to search for the blacks, while Wills, unable to move, lay in a crude hut built of branches. He was nearing the end when he wrote: 'I can only look out, like Mr Micawber, for something to turn up.' In the last letter he wrote, which was to his father, he says: 'I think to live about four or five days.'

Burke was not in much better condition than Wills, and the two men had not travelled very far when he began to complain bitterly of fierce pains in his back and legs, and on the second day he collapsed, unable to go on. Just before he died, he wrote a note for King to take with him. 'King has behaved nobly. He has stayed with me to the last, and placed a pistol in my hand, leaving me lying on the surface as I wished. R.O'Hara Burke – Cooper's Creek, 28 June.'

King wandered for a number of days in search of the natives. Finally, he stumbled across a hut containing a supply of nardoo from which the Aborigines obtained flour to make into cakes. There was enough to last him for a fortnight, so he rested there for a few days and gathered his strength. Then he returned to the camp where they had left Wills. Wills lay where they had left him, but he was dead and had been for some time and a group of natives had taken most of his clothes.

All alone and very close to total despair, King hung round the camp for a few more days. He then followed the footprints left in the sand by the natives who had taken Wills's clothes, and eventually tracked them down. When this scarecrow of a white man, obviously close to death, staggered into their camp, the natives fed him and looked after him with great

compassion. He was welcomed into the tribe and nursed back to a much healthier condition, but the native diet was inadequate and he slowly deteriorated again. He had been staying with the Aborigines for about a month when one of them who had been up the creek on a fishing expedition ran into the camp shouting, 'White fellows! White fellows!' The native led King across the creek towards a group of horsemen, part of a rescue party sent out from Melbourne.

Overnight King became a national hero. Everyone wanted to shake the hand of the man who had come back from the dead. The Melbourne *Herald* wrote: 'John King is regarded with feelings similar to those which made people say of Dante, "There goes a man who has been in Hades".'

A contemporary engraving of the public funeral in Melbourne of the explorers Burke and Wills

CHAPTER 7

Escape from the Deep

*The door flew open.
He was flung backwards. As he hit
the deck he saw a cascade of sea water
rushing into the boat through
the torpedo tube.*

'All gone forward'. 'All gone aft'.

The heavy steel hawsers hit the water, and HMS *Thetis* slipped away from the dock, her powerful propellers churning the murky waters of the Mersey as she headed towards the open sea. It was 11am on 1 June 1939, and Britain's latest 'T' class submarine, her brand new ensign bravely fluttering from the conning tower, was about to commence her first diving trials. It was a glorious summer's day. The sun shimmered on the flat calm of Liverpool Bay and the conditions were perfect for her first dive, to be made in only 42 metres of water and in sight of land. It was to be a normal slow dive to check the diving machinery.

Thetis steaming out into the calm of Liverpool Bay to make her first dive

Below decks there was an air of festivity. For the fifty-three officers and ratings of the crew it was one step nearer to officially accepting *Thetis* from the shipbuilders, Cammell Laird. After months of inactivity around the shipyard they were anxious to join a sea-going submarine flotilla. The trials routine was well established and it was unthinkable that anything could go wrong. Cammell Laird had a reputation for building sound, reliable ships. As well as the crew there were fifty passengers on board: admiralty officials who had come up from London to witness the trials, officers from other submarines being built in the yard who were

taking the opportunity to see how the boat behaved under water, and Captain H. P. K. Oram, the commanding officer of the flotilla to which *Thetis* would be attached. There were also a number of men from the shipyard who would operate the diving machinery under the orders of the naval officers, this being the normal routine before a new submarine was officially accepted by the Admiralty. For the passengers it was a day out, a welcome relief from their usual humdrum routine, and the crowded boat rang with their laughter as they picnicked on beer and sandwiches.

One man was far from happy. Up on the bridge, *Thetis*'s commander, Lieutenant Commander 'Sam' Bolus, could not rid himself of a premonition of disaster. The words of Robert Ostler kept returning to his mind; 'I wish you didn't have to go, sir.' Ostler, one of his engineers and an experienced, level-headed submariner, had developed a superstitious dread of *Thetis*. He refused to sail in her and had been transferred to another submarine. Sam Bolus shook off his gloomy thoughts and scanned the horizon for HMS *Grebecock*, the tug whose duty it was to follow the submarine and keep away any passing ship who might endanger her. He spotted her at the correct diving position, 24 kilometres north of Great Ormes Head. On board *Grebecock* was a submarine officer, Lieutenant Coltart, whose job it was to watch the dive from the surface. He had already agreed with Sam Bolus how the

81

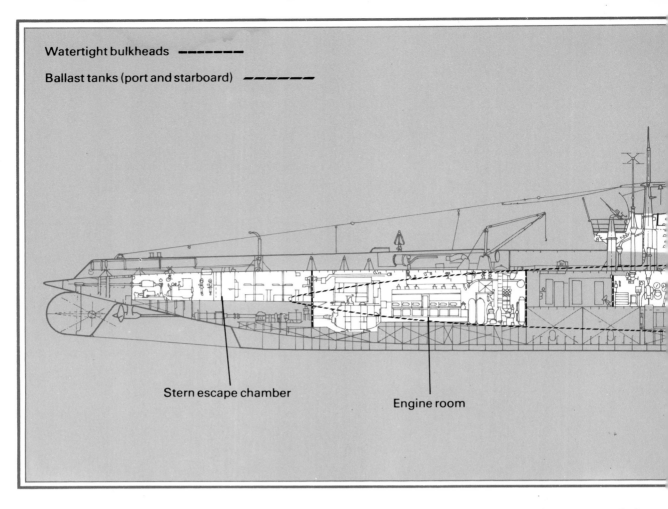

Watertight bulkheads ⎯ ⎯ ⎯ ⎯ ⎯

Ballast tanks (port and starboard) ⎯ ⎯ ⎯ ⎯ ⎯

Stern escape chamber

Engine room

dive should be carried out. *Thetis* was to remain throughout at periscope depth as it was impossible to keep radio contact with her while she was submerged. *Thetis* was to fly a red flag from her periscope so that she could be seen more clearly.

It was just before 1.30 pm. Sam Bolus waved to Lieutenant Coltart and gave the order to clear the bridge and stand by to dive. As the last one down, he slammed the conning tower hatch and ordered: 'Prepare to dive'.

'Flood ballast tanks.'

Thousands of litres of sea water rushed into the submarine, but nothing happened! *Thetis* was travelling at 10 knots, but she was hardly going under at all. Ten minutes passed, then twenty, then thirty, but still the conning tower remained half out of the water. At this stage of her trials *Thetis* had no torpedoes aboard, but their weight should have been compensated for by filling two of her torpedo tubes (the bottom two numbered five and six) with water.

However, it was obvious that she was very light forward and not diving correctly. The commander sent forward Lieutenant Woods, the torpedo officer, to see if in fact the two tubes had been flooded.

The torpedo 'tube space', right up in the bow, was the smallest and most cramped compartment in *Thetis*. Almost half the length of the torpedo tubes extended back into the compartment, hardly leaving room for the four man crew to operate them. To the rear of the tubes, hardly a metre away, was the collision bulkhead which had two oval watertight doors in line with the port and starboard sets of torpedo tubes. There was a heavy door at the back of each tube through which the torpedoes were loaded, with a number engraved on a brass plate. Reading from top to bottom, they were numbered according to naval practice, 1,3,5 on the starboard side, 2,4,6 on the port side. At the other end of the tube there was another door, the bow cap. This, opened

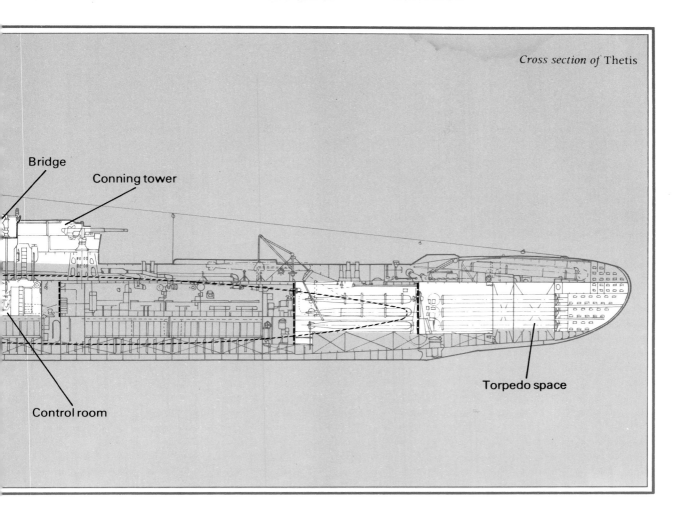

Bridge

Conning tower

Torpedo space

Control room

straight into the sea and was always kept secured until the torpedo was about to be fired. If the bow cap and rear door were opened at the same time the sea would flood into the boat, with disastrous results. There was a test cock on the rear door of the tube to guard against this happening. If this was opened when the tube was full of water the pressure would drive out a thin jet of water. If the tube was only partially filled only a few drops would come out, a 'slop of water'. If no water came out it was safe to open the tube.

The torpedo 'stowage space', the largest compartment on the boat was directly behind the collision bulkhead. The 'reload' torpedoes were stowed here, with ample room to examine and overhaul them, and if necessary for maintenance, haul back the torpedoes already in the tubes.

Lieutenant Woods hurried through the watertight door. Two torpedo ratings were already there; Chief Petty Officer Mitchell, the

'Torpedo Gunner's Mate', and Leading Seaman Hambrook. On the surface the watertight doors are kept firmly closed, but during diving one must always remain open. So that afternoon on *Thetis* the port door was hooked back against the bulkhead. The torpedo officer lifted the test cock on number six tube and a few drops of water slopped out indicating that the tube was partly full. No water at all seeped from number five. He reported by telephone to the control room and awaited orders to fill the tubes by opening the bow caps. They had been submerged for forty-five minutes and still no order had been given. So Lieutenant Woods decided to carry out his programme for the dive; to check for any signs of leakage from the sea. Sometimes in a new submarine the outside pressure and forward movement of the boat forced a few drops of water through the bow caps. He had only to open the rear doors, one by one, shine his flashlight up the empty tube and see if any water was seeping in.

He ordered Leading Seaman Hambrook to open tubes 1 and 2, then shone in his flashlight and found them dry. 3 and 4 were also quite dry. He was more cautious with the bottom two which were supposed to be flooded. Once again a 'slop of water' came out of number six, so he decided to leave it alone and moved across to number five. He lifted the test cock; nothing came out, so he ordered Hambrook to open the door. The seaman heaved on the lever, which moved a little way and then stuck. Woods leaned over to help him and the two men threw all their weight onto the lever; the door flew open. Woods was flung backwards. As he hit the deck he saw a cascade of sea water rushing into the boat through the torpedo tube.

'Mitchell, tell the control room. Number five tube open to the sea. For God's sake blow main ballast,' shouted Woods. Precious seconds were wasted as he tried to drag Hambrook, who was stunned by the accident, across the sill of the port door. Willing hands pulled them through to the next compartment, but already the sea was boiling over the sill into the stowage space, reverbrating like thunder in the confined area.

The pressure of water rushing through the torpedo tube throws Woods backwards

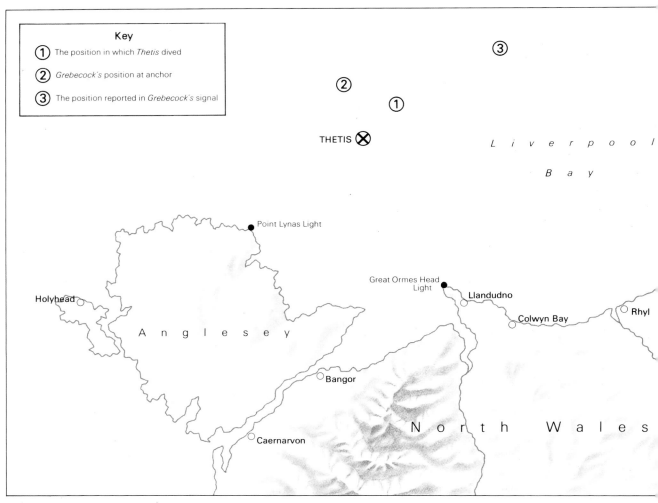

Key

① The position in which *Thetis* dived

② *Grebecock's* position at anchor

③ The position reported in *Grebecock's* signal

THETIS ⊗

L i v e r p o o l

B a y

Point Lynas Light

Great Ormes Head Light

Llandudno

Colwyn Bay

Rhyl

Holyhead

A n g l e s e y

Bangor

Caernarvon

N o r t h   W a l e s

Above the noise they could hear the air being blown into the ballast tanks, but the bows of the boat were dropping alarmingly. They tried desperately to close the watertight door, pushing it against the rising water. Suddenly the lights went out and they were in total darkness. Still the door would not shut. Woods was afraid that the sea water would reach the electric batteries in the next compartment and release a deadly flow of chlorine. If this happened it would roll relentlessly through the ship, killing everyone on board; Woods ordered everyone behind the next watertight door.

The men hurried up the now crazily sloping deck, running into each other in the dark. They reached the next compartment, then shut the door and slammed on the clips. White-faced they stared at each other. *Thetis* was rapidly sinking, bows first. In the control room the commander clung to the periscope housing, his eyes riveted to the depth gauge. The compressed air which roared into the ballast tanks was forcing out the sea water and the boat began to level out.

'Thank God,' thought Sam Bolus.

Very slowly, her bows began to drop and she began sinking again faster than ever. *Thetis* was head down at 40 degrees when she hit the sea bed. The bows sank into the mud, 48 metres below the surface.

'Engines full astern,' shouted Sam Bolus.

The boat shuddered violently, but the racing engines were unable to drag her loose. She was too firmly embedded in the mud.

'Stop main motors.'

'Stop blowing.'

The sudden quiet was unnerving. A shiver of fear ran through the boat, as the stern slowly sank until *Thetis* was at an angle of only 5 degrees. What had gone wrong? Why had the bow cap been left open? Why hadn't the test

But as he said afterwards at the enquiry, he was not particularly worried. It was, after all, a slow dive and he thought that perhaps the submarine commander was being more cautious than usual. Suddenly he saw the bows drop, and *Thetis* disappeared under the calm waters of the Bay. He was still not uneasy for these things often happened. He did not know it, but he was watching the end of *Thetis*.

Sam Bolus and Captain Oram hurried towards the bows of the submarine. The crew watched in nervous silence as they passed. The experienced 'submariners' knew only too well the meaning of the sudden rush of wind through the boat. The two officers found a badly shocked Woods by the door to the stowage space. They looked through the thick glass observation window in the door and saw that the compartment was already half-full of water. Soon it would be completely full. They both realised that they would never be able to raise *Thetis* with that amount of water in her. At a meeting of officers they decided that they should pump the water out of the stern ballast tanks. This should cause the stern to rise, and with any luck the stern escape chamber would be above the surface. Everyone must help, crew and civilians alike. It was now past 5pm, the time scheduled for the end of the dive.

On board *Grebecock* Lieutenant Coltart stood watching the spot where *Thetis* had gone under. The red flag had disappeared. He wondered whether Bolus, despite the agreement to stay at periscope depth, had changed his plans. *Grebecock* steered in the direction *Thetis* should have taken, every minute pulling further away from the stricken boat. At 2.30pm there was no sign of the red flag. At 3pm there was still no sign of it. Coltart began to feel uneasy. At 4pm still no red flag had appeared. He was now very uneasy. He decided to send a cautious radio message to base. The radio on *Grebecock* could only reach as far as a station in the north of England. From there any message would have to go by regular Post Office telegram service to the submarine base at Gosport, on the south coast. A message was tapped out. 'How long should *Thetis* remain under water?'

At Gosport the telegram was given to a delivery boy. By a cruel stroke of luck his

cock worked? These and a dozen other questions sprang to mind, but everyone was frightened to ask the one vital question, would they get out? A marker buoy was sent up which would stay on the surface joined to the submarine by a wire. The commander was not too concerned. He felt that their marker would be spotted before dark, and the *Grebecock* was somewhere up there. His main anxiety arose from the fact that the air in a 'T' class submarine was expected to last for 36 hours with a crew of 53. Now 103 people had to breathe the same amount of air. How long would it last?

At 1.30pm, Lieutenant Coltart saw the bridge of *Thetis* cleared; his old friend Sam waved to him before he went below. Seconds later he saw water spuming around the submarine as air rushed out of the ballast tanks and sea water poured in along the length of the ship. Her electric motors were pushing her forward, but he was surprised that she was not going under.

bicycle had a puncture and he stopped to mend it before delivering the telegram. It was not delivered until 6.15pm. When the Admiral, the Chief of Staff, Submarines, received the telegram he sprang into action. He lifted the telephone and quickly began issuing his orders.

Aboard *Thetis* the night dragged on. As the water was pumped out the stern began to rise gradually. Slowly the time passed, 9pm, 10pm, 11pm. By midnight it was difficult to breathe. The stale air had already lasted them ten hours. How much longer would it last? The stern of the ship continued to rise. By 4am she was at an angle of 60 degrees. 50 tons of fuel and 10 tons of water had been pumped out. Now most of the men were too weak to stand, and they sprawled about on the sharply sloping deck, made sleepy by the increasing amount of carbon dioxide. They lay taking in deep breaths of foul air. Their eyes watered and many were sick.

Everyone felt tired and it was almost too much effort to move. At a meeting it was agreed that Captain Oram and Lieutenant Woods should attempt to escape from the submarine with a written report drawn up by the Engineering Officer, giving a full account of the conditions on *Thetis*. It also contained information which would assist any rescue operation. This was carefully wrapped in a waterproof oilskin packet and attached to the wrist of Lieutenant Woods in case he was drowned making his way to the surface.

The two men in the tiny escape chamber pray that they may be able to save themselves and the others on board

The two men painfully dragged themselves aft up the steeply sloping deck to the stern escape chamber. This was small with thick metal walls which reached from the deck to the outer hull of the submarine. In the deck head or ceiling there was a heavy hatch which opened directly to the sea. The chamber was entered through a small watertight door in the side, which had a thick glass observation window above it. When the chamber was flooded, the pressure became the same as the sea outside. The hatch could then be opened and anyone inside would rush to the surface helped by the air caught in the top of the chamber.

Two of the crew helped Oram and Woods crawl into the escape chamber. They were already breathing more easily, having donned the Davis Escape Apparatus. The rich oxygen quickly revitalised their blood. There was more than enough oxygen to see them safely to the surface.

The watertight door slammed shut. Just before it shut they heard tapping on the hull in Morse code. It read, 'C O M E   O U T' Although the escape chamber itself was under water there was 5.4 metres of the stern above the surface. Surely it would be easy to effect a rescue of the entire crew of *Thetis*?

The two of them were alone in the escape chamber. It was a very close fit and was also deathly quiet. A minute passed. They wondered if anything had gone wrong. Then the water began coming into the chamber. It was around their feet then slowly it began to rise. It swirled waist high until it reached their chests. As it crept towards their mouths they began to wonder whether the Davis Escape Apparatus was foolproof. The only time before that they had experienced this was in a 5 metre training tank at submarine school, and in the case of Captain Oram that was many, many years ago. The chamber was now full of water and thankfully they could still breathe. They tried to open the hatch, but the wheel was new and stiff and they were pitifully weak. Frantically they pulled at it. At last it gave and they shot to the surface and safety. The time was 7.30am.

At Weymouth, holiday-makers were basking in the evening sun. The threat of war seemed a long way away, despite the eight 'Tribal' class destroyers anchored in the bay. There was a sudden clatter of anchor chains and the sixth destroyer flotilla was under way. Black smoke belching from their funnels they raced towards the west. That night the evening papers carried banner headlines, 'THETIS MISSING.'

The Admiral, Submarines, had acted swiftly; as well as the Tribal class destroyers, believed to be the fastest in the world, another destroyer HMS *Brazen* was ploughing through the Irish Sea towards Liverpool Bay. At 5.40pm four aircraft took off to join in the search, but their airfield was 240 kilometres away. *Brazen* and the aircraft arrived in the area at approximately the same time, not until 9pm, by which time it was getting dark. The planes were forced to

return to base, but *Brazen* searched all night, and at 7.25am *Thetis* was sighted. *Brazen*'s commander could hardly believe his eyes: there was the submarine with 5.4 metres of her stern above the surface of the sea.

'Radio all ships' he ordered, '*Thetis* found.' The crew of the submarine had been under water for eighteen hours. As *Brazen* closed with *Thetis* two heads suddenly bobbed to the surface. It was Captain Oram and Lieutenant Woods. They were both too weak to speak but

Thetis is finally found. Oram and Woods, although too weak to speak, indicate the engineer's report of the frightful conditions below

Woods struggled to hold up his arm, to which was tied the Engineering Officer's report.

'*From* Thetis. *On the bottom. Depth 48 metres. Tube space and stowage space full of water. Number five bow cap and inside door open to the sea. Air must be pumped into the submarine to save her. A diver must close the hatch to the deck more closely, or the air will escape. Look out for men escaping through the stern escape chamber.*'

At 10am two more heads appeared; Leading Stoker Arnold and Frank Shaw, a Cammell Laird man. They were the only other men to escape. They told a dreadful tale of the conditions aboard *Thetis*. Many of the crew were already dead and four others had been drowned in the escape chamber, when one man panicked and pulled the face masks off the others.

Down in the submarine there were several more half-hearted attempts to escape, but the men were far too weak to open the hatch. The last attempt was made at 3pm. It was a tragic failure. The wrong door was opened and the sea rushed into the engine room. Very few on *Thetis* knew what happened.

CHAPTER 8

Billy Bishop meets the Red Baron

*Head-on they raced towards
each other on a direct collision
course at a combined approach speed of
320 kilometres an hour.*

The Dawn Patrol straggled out of the mess at first light and made their way across the dew-soaked grass to the single-seater Nieuports parked ready for take off. The Flight Commander was Lieutenant 'Billy' Bishop, a Canadian who already had thirteen confirmed victories to his credit and was to go on to register seventy two by the end of the war. He climbed into the cockpit of his combat machine and made last minute checks.

'Contact, sir?' called the mechanic standing at the propeller.

'Contact.'

The click of an electric ignition switch sounded in the early morning quiet. The propeller was swung over and the engine started with a roar. Once or twice it coughed and spluttered, but soon ran sweetly, 'hitting' just right on its multiple cylinders. Bishop throttled down to a quiet purr and signalled to the aircraftman to pull away the chocks from under the wheels. Slowly the Nieuport taxied across the field and headed into the wind for take off. Bishop opened the throttle and the machine rushed forward gathering speed. He pulled back the 'joystick', felt the tail lift and was airborne. It was 30 April 1917, and the flight was off on patrol from an airfield somewhere in France.

The planes took up formation and flew east towards the German lines. Bishop spotted the black crosses of an enemy machine below him, waved the rest of the flight on and went into a steep dive. The nose of his Nieuport went beyond the vertical and he was flung forward, striking his head against the little windscreen.

His burst of machine-gun fire went wide, and the German pilot, by frantically flinging his aircraft sideways, was able to escape. As he climbed away Bishop realised that he was alone. The rest of his flight were nowhere to be seen, but in the distance and above him were two monstrous German machines. He approached them and realised that they were the new three-seater Gotha bombers, which were later to suffer severe losses when bombing London. He pulled sharply back on his joystick and raced

upwards making for the 'blind spot' of the leading German.

Bishop later wrote: 'We must have made a ludicrous picture, little me under the huge Hun. I felt like a mosquito chasing a wasp.' As he closed on the German the other Gotha came at him in a slow spiral, seeming 'to open up with a whole battery of machine-guns'. He hung on, grimly determined, until, at point-blank range he opened fire. He shot off fifteen rounds before his Lewis gun jammed. He could do nothing

Billy Bishop preparing for take-off. Owing to the small number of men and planes in World War I, fliers had to follow an exhausting and punishing flying schedule

with it in the air, so was forced to break off the attack and return to his airfield, which was a few kilometres away. Only a couple of minutes after landing the gun was cleared and he was once again in the air, climbing sharply to gain height. Furious at himself for missing the chance of bringing down one of the new

93

Gothas, he was determined to add to his string of thirteen victories as quickly as possible. As he flew out of some light cloud he sighted three Halberstadts about 3 kilometres away and 300 metres below him. These two-seater reconnaissance planes were busy 'spotting' for the German artillery.

He banked sharply, and went into a dive aiming his machine at the middle one of the three Halberstadts. With the wind whistling through his struts and tearing at his silk scarf, he plummeted down on the enemy at over 300 kilometres an hour. He was well above the Germans when he was spotted by the observer of the rear plane. Immediately, all hell was let loose as three twin machine-guns loosed a hail of lead in his direction. Holes began to appear in the flimsy fabric of his machine; they were shooting well. His return gunfire drilled a line of holes across the upper wing of the centre Halberstadt, and although no damage was done, the Germans turned as one and made off in the direction of their own lines. It was unusual for three planes, with heavier armaments, to run from a single fighter.

Billy Bishop followed, manoeuvring to get into the 'killing' position behind the tail of the enemy. Pilots of single-seater fighters had to be constantly on the look-out in every direction, particularly over their shoulders as they had no observer to watch out for them. This was a golden rule to Bishop, and his care in maintaining such vigilance was one reason he was able to survive the war. Today was no exception. This was just as well, for 2 kilometres ahead and above his starboard wing, he noticed five bright scarlet planes racing towards him. They were single-seater Albatrosses of the 'Richthofen Circus', the cream of the German Air Force. Manfred von Richthofen, the 'Red Baron', was the greatest ace of them all, with eighty victories to his credit at the time he was shot down in flames. Bishop realised his danger and climbed to gain height, relying on his Nieuport to outclimb the Albatrosses. He was well above the Germans when he tilted the nose of his machine and screamed down towards the centre of the scarlet formation, guns chattering. A few metres above them he jerked back his stick and zoomed upwards almost vertically. The German aces were taken unawares. They

had expected him to dive straight through their formation, and were already banking to follow him down. Twice he dived down on the Germans, fired a burst and pulled out. These

Bishop adding another victory to his credit, only just manages to manoeuvre himself out of trouble

novel tactics were too much for them; they broke formation and scattered.

Bishop now looked round for the treacherous two-seaters which had led him into the trap. There they were, once again artillery spotting, confident that the 'Red Devils' had dealt with the troublesome Britisher. Their first hint of danger came with the chatter of the Canadian's gun as he dived at them out of the sun. The observer of the centre Halberstadt swung his twin machine guns round to bear on the Nieuport, but a line of bullet holes flickered along the fuselage of his machine and he slumped forward, mortally wounded. The Halberstadt dived away with the Canadian on its tail. There was another burst and the German was spinning down, out of control. It crashed in a sheet of flame behind the enemy lines. Bishop, following closely behind, was met with a blanket of fire, his machine surrounded by white puffs of smoke as the anti-aircraft shells burst around him. He zoomed upwards but ran into more trouble. The five scarlet scouts had regrouped and were heading for the British lines on the look-out for lone British artillery machines. He followed his previous tactics, refusing to mix in the middle of them, and disgusted, they turned away east towards their own lines. It was nearly lunch-time and he was running short of ammunition, so he turned for home. On his way back he had a skirmish with a further two German artillery spotters, but at his first burst, they sped away. After a time they plucked up courage and returned to their artillery spotting. Bishop manoeuvred himself between the Halberstadts and their own lines and commenced to attack the leading machine from directly in front.

They were within 180 metres of each other when Bishop opened fire. He could see his tracer bullets smacking into the enemy machine. Then the German's guns began to chatter, the bullets humming through the struts

of the Nieuport. Head-on, they raced towards each other on a direct collision course at a combined approach speed of over 320 kilometres an hour. Their trigger fingers were pressed hard down, and bullets were screeching off the metal cowlings. 27 metres and they were both still holding course, then, in the words of Bishop, '. . . much to my relief, be it confessed, the Hun dived, and I thought I had hit him. I turned quickly, but in doing so lost sight of him completely. Then a second later I saw him, some distance away; going down in a slight glide quite under control, but I think badly hit.'

Combat in the air during the First World War was a very individual affair; fliers on each side would often choose one target on the other and pursue him mercilessly

He had hardly any ammunition left when he once again took up course for his airfield, but just short of base he spotted another enemy two-seater and dived to the attack. Almost vertical, he saved his few remaining rounds until he was within point-blank range. Meanwhile the German observer had opened fire and bullets were 'biting' off scraps of the Nieuport's flimsy structure. The enemy banked and Bishop zoomed past, but pulling quickly out of the dive he found the 'blind spot', directly under the Halberstadt, and fired his final few rounds. But he was not shooting at his best that morning so the German was able to go into a shallow glide and the Canadian saw him land in a field just behind his own lines. It had been an eventful morning. Completely out of ammunition, Bishop landed and strolled into the mess for his midday meal; as he nonchalently put it: 'Two or three batteries took "bites" at me as I crossed the line for luncheon.'

In the afternoon he took off with his squadron commander who was a veteran pilot. For twenty minutes they patrolled the lines, then headed into enemy territory. Presently, well to the south they saw five Albatross combat scouts and went after them, the major way out in front. Before they came into range Bishop glanced to his right; there were four scarlet Albatrosses, blissfully unaware of the Nieuports. Bishop felt a quick stab of fear for the leading pilot was the 'Red Baron' himself, Rittmeister Manfred von Richthofen. Three of his best men were with him. These men were the top aces of the German Air Force.

The Major waved to Bishop to follow him, and went in to the attack despite the odds, and opened fire on the rear machine from behind. In a flash the German biplane banked and making a lightning turn, came back at the major with its machine guns blazing and passing within a metre of the Nieuport. Bishop got in two sharp bursts at the Baron, then the air was a whirling mass of aircraft and roaring guns. Smoking bullets hummed past and thwacked into the wood of the Nieuport's superstructure. For the first time in his combat career he knew real fear. He fired every time he saw a flash of red in his sights, carefully avoiding the silver of his commander's machine. This situation was vastly different from that of the morning. These German aces were top fliers. Round and round they circled, manoeuvring for position, firing quick bursts and banking away out of trouble and often choked by the cordite fumes blown back from their own guns. For one nerve-racking minute Bishop's guns jammed. He wildly flung his machine about from side to side, 'fussing' with the weapon to get it right. Just as he cleared his gun Richthofen flashed across him and he gave him a short burst. Four triplanes from a Royal Naval squadron joined in the fight and Richthofen decided to call it a day. He made off at top speed for his base, signalling his flight to follow.

Bishop looked round for his commander, but he was nowhere in sight. He circled the area for

five minutes then made for home with a heavy heart. It was obvious that the major had fallen victim to the formidable 'Richthofen Circus'. On his way back to base he sighted another machine and took up an attacking position, then to his joy recognised his commander, and side by side they flew back. Once down they were horrified to see just how badly they had been shot up. Strips of fabric hung down from the fuselage and wing, and dents showed where bullets had ricocheted off metal. Bishop turned cold when he realised that one group of seven bullets had passed within 3 centimetres of his body. But as he summed it up: 'It had been a close shave, but a wonderful, soul-stirring fight.'

In spite of the odds, Bishop and his commander decide to take on the Germans. They are luckily aided by Royal Naval triplanes.
Inset: Above: *Billy Bishop.* Below: *the Red Baron, Manfred von Richthofen*

CHAPTER 9

Conquest of Everest

The ridge was a daunting sight. Steep and narrow, the rock beneath the coating of snow and ice had been eroded over the years into a brittle mass that could break away under the climber's feet at any time.

Furiously the two men swung their ice-axes, chipping out a platform in the packed snow and rock of the narrow sloping ledge. This ledge, high above the South Col of Everest and only a few hundred metres from the summit, was exposed to the fierce wind that gusted across the face of the mountain. Overhead towered the ridge that led to the main summit. Edmund Hillary and Tensing Norkay, who were the second string assault team of John Hunt's 1953 Everest expedition, were setting up their final camp before the attack on the summit the next morning. It was a race against time. It meant certain death from exposure to be caught at night without shelter in a sub-zero temperature. Both men were determined to be the first to gaze from the summit of Everest, and in preparation for the moment, Tensing carried the flags of the United Nations, Britain, India and Nepal, wrapped round his ice-axe.

As they struggled with the madly-flapping tent, they realised only too well that their survival depended on it being securely anchored to the ledge. At this altitude every movement was a tremendous effort. It took them over two hours to pitch their orange nylon tent, which at lower altitudes would have taken them only fifteen minutes. After two hours of bitter cold, their minds were clouded through lack of oxygen, and they found it difficult to cope with even the most simple problems. The aluminium tent pegs bent when they tried to drive them into the frozen ground, so Hillary used the empty oxygen cylinders, tightly packed with snow, to hold down the guy ropes. Meanwhile Tensing lashed the tent to a jutting outcrop of rock.

Gratefully the two men crawled inside, lit the kerosene cooker and crouched over its warmth. A cooker, 'in good working order' was indispensable for survival, and could mean the difference between success and failure. It supplied the warmth necessary to keep climbers alive in sub-zero temperatures; it allowed them to eat hot food, and equally important, it was vital for melting snow to provide drinking water. It was impossible to include fresh water in the 30 kilo pack of supplies carried by members of support teams.

Physical effort in heavy, protective clothing causes climbers to perspire at an alarming rate, and to replace this loss of moisture from their bodies they have to drink at least 4.5 litres of lemon juice and water laced with enormous amounts of sugar which is burned up to provide energy every day.

Hastily they 'brewed up' and prepared an energy-packed meal, starting with hot chicken noodle soup. This was followed by sardines, dates, biscuits and a tin of apricots, which had frozen solid and had to be levered out of the can. Hillary checked their oxygen supply and found that there was not nearly as much as he had expected. It looked as if they would have to spend a miserable, near-sleepless night. Climbers find it very difficult to sleep in the thin atmosphere of high altitudes without the aid of oxygen. Allowing seven hours oxygen for the climb, this left them only two spells of two hours each during the night. The two men took it in turns to sleep. While one slept the other brewed up, so throughout the night they had a constant supply of hot, sweet tea. If the wind increased in strength and prevented them from starting at first light, or if the climb took longer than expected, the three small cylinders of oxygen would be insufficient and they would fail in their attempt. Outside, the howling wind did its best to tear the tent from its precarious moorings.

It seemed unlikely that any attempt on the summit would be possible the following day,

Hillary and Tensing checking their equipment in preparation for their assault upon Everest

and Hillary and Tensing resigned themselves to the possibility of having to return to Camp VIII to report another failure. Surprisingly, these two men from very different backgrounds and parts of the world had a great deal in common. Both had a burning ambition to beat Everest and reach the highest point ever climbed by man. This was unusual in a Sherpa, for although the Sherpas put their heart and soul into the enterprise, they usually found it difficult to understand this urge on the part of Europeans to get to the top. Tensing, a mountain man, had spent his whole life at high altitudes. Some Nepalese villages in the shadow of the Himalayas are built at over 5,000 metres, and he was completely acclimatised to high altitudes. He already shared with a Swiss, Raymond Lambert, the distinction of being the first men to get within 300 metres of the summit of Everest.

His companion, Edmund Hillary, a New Zealand bee-keeper, was one of the most experienced ice-climbers in the world. He had been brought up to climb the glaciers of his native country, and had developed an individual technique which made him an ideal choice to lead an assault on the ice-encrusted face of the main summit. These two had perfect confidence in each other and pairing them together as a team was a stroke of genius on the part of John Hunt.

The meal over, the two men lay fully clothed in their sleeping bags, busily turning over in their minds the crowded events of the past few days. On 26 May, a break in the almost continuous bad weather allowed Evans and Bourdillon, Hunt's first string, to make the initial assault. They were to climb by way of the long south-east ridge to the South Summit; and from there it was less than 100 metres to the true summit of Everest. For much of the time cloud hid the climbers from the anxious watchers in Camp VIII. In mid-afternoon during a break in the cloud Evans and Bourdillon were spotted; two tiny figures silhouetted against the South Summit.

'They're up! By God, they're up!'

With only under 100 metres to go it seemed certain that Everest had at last been conquered. Then cloud plumes streamed from the summit completely obscuring the climbers. Later it

cleared again, but to the dismay of the watchers, Evans and Bourdillon were slowly moving downward. Something must have gone very wrong, and a party from the camp hurried to meet them. Evans and Bourdillon staggered towards the camp party, completely exhausted, their clothes and beards stiff with ice. They had been climbing since early morning and despite trouble with their oxygen sets they had made the South Summit, 8,610 metres high, the highest point anyone had ever climbed. But one glance at the last short distance had convinced them that they would be lucky to make it in their condition. This final lap appeared to offer the most difficult climbing of the entire attempt. It was also doubtful whether they had sufficient oxygen left to make the summit, then descend safely. Reluctantly, bitterly disappointed, and not without some argument, the two men had sensibly turned their backs on the summit and started down for Camp VIII.

Now it was the turn of Hillary and Tensing to make the assault; but next day a blizzard swept the area which made a further attempt impossible. Recently, due to the approach of the monsoon season, it had begun to cloud over in the afternoon and snow heavily for two or three hours. 'White-outs' a combination of cloud and the brilliant white of the snow and ice, made any sense of direction impossible, and were

Evans and Bourdillon, utterly exhausted and disappointed, after their unsuccessful attempt upon the summit

Mt. Everest
8.840m

South Peak
Camp IX

Camp VIII
7.925m

Lhotse
8.501m

Geneva Spur

Traverse

Changtse
7.535m

North Col

Camp VII
7.315m

Bergschrund

Camp VI

Nuptse
7.827m

Camp V

Western Cwm

Camp IV
6,462m

Rongbuk Glacier

Camp III

Lho La
6.096m

Icefall

Camp II

Base Camp (Camp I)
5,456m

Khumbu Glacier

◁N

dreaded by mountaineers climbing at these heights. Many an experienced climber had slipped to his death down an ice cliff or crevasse while wandering aimlessly in a 'white-out'. In moving from one tent to another, Hillary was bowled over by the wind and had to complete the journey on hands and knees. Next day the blizzard had abated, and although there was still a fierce wind it was decided to move supplies and oxygen and set up a camp site just below the summit. Hillary and Tensing would make the second attempt on the summit from there.

8,700 metres high, the highest mountain in the world, Everest had always been a lure and fascination to climbers. As early as 1921 the first expeditions began to reconnoitre the mountain, and in 1922 the first serious assault was attempted. From thereon there was attempt after attempt. Each one ended in failure. Lives were lost, but still the unconquerable mountain drew climbers like a magnet. Before 1952, all attempts to climb Everest had been made from the north, the Tibetan side of the mountain. Mountaineers were forbidden to climb from the south, the Nepalese side. But when the Chinese occupied Tibet they closed the borders and refused permission to all foreign Everest expeditions. However, a change of heart on the part of Nepal made it possible, for the first time, to make an assault from the south. Permission was just granted to a Swiss team in 1952, to be followed by the British venture in 1953.

In the final attempt of the Swiss expedition in 1952, a mountain guide, Raymond Lambert, accompanied by Tensing of Hunt's expedition, nearly succeeded, when they got within 300 metres of the summit. This valiant effort was even more remarkable in light of the fact that the two men made the final assault without the assistance of a support team. They had no food or cooker and were inadequately clothed. Despite the opinion of many informed climbers who thought that the mountain would never yield, the 1953 British expedition set out in March 1953, under a 42-year-old army officer, John Hunt. This expedition, was better equipped than ever before, and armed with all the experience of previous attempts, was determined to succeed. If planning, training and organisation carried any weight, they would.

John Hunt was an admirable choice as leader. Always leading from the front he set the other members of the expedition an example they were only too eager to follow. He was ably backed up by his expedition secretary, Charles Wylie, who was a fine organiser with a stable, unflappable personality. He was also a first class climber, who could 'climb high'. Climbing ability alone was not enough when tackling 8,700 metres; men had to be able to 'climb high'. Many were unable to adjust themselves

to such altitudes, and still climb. Being a Gurkha officer, Wylie understood, liked and respected the Nepalese Sherpas and was able to get the best out of them. As well as Sherpa porters there were a number of Sherpa 'Tigers', who were seasoned mountain men experienced in Himalayan climbing. They would be used in the final stages on the summit in support teams. All, that is, except Tensing who was highly thought of as an 'assault man'.

Some purists still regarded the use of oxygen as unsporting, but it was generally realised from the very first attempt in 1922 that without oxygen it would be impossible to climb Everest. The Hunt expedition paid special attention to the breathing equipment. They realised the importance of a good supply of rich oxygen over the last vital few hundred metres. Tom Bourdillon and his father had come up with a

The base camp for the expedition, at Thyangboche monastery, which is set in incomparable scenery

new close circuit breathing set. Instead of a mixture of oxygen and air, the climber breathed neat oxygen; the waste carbon dioxide was recycled again. It was as yet untested at Himalayan altitudes, but it was hoped that it would go a long way in helping to achieve those last few desperate metres to the top.

The team consisted of John Hunt and nine other climbers. Two were New Zealanders and the rest Englishmen. And there were also the 'Tigers'. In addition a doctor, physiologist and film cameraman accompanied the expedition. They all met for the first time in the Nepalese capital of Katmandu. Here they agreed to set up a chain of base camps leading to the final assault on the summit. Hunt was convinced that the key to a successful assault lay in the use of support teams and an intense effort to become acclimatised to altitude. The actual climb itself was not a difficult one. It was more a question of stamina and the ability to work and climb at 8,700 metres. Hunt reasoned that an assault team would have a greater chance of success if it were to attack from a position on the face of the summit already provisioned with equipment and supplies ferried there by a support team. Carrying a 30 kilos load at this height was an arduous business and relieving an assault team of this chore meant that they would be comparatively fresh when making the final effort.

In March 1953, they set off on their march to the first base camp, the monastery of Thyangboche. For seventeen days the long caravan, of 350 porters, both male and female, carrying nearly 12 tonnes of supplies, wended its way across Nepal towards the Everest group. The villages in the foothills seemed to hang from the sides of the mountains. The villagers shared their two-storeyed houses with their cattle. The family lived upstairs, the cattle downstairs, providing a primitive but effective form of central-heating. Eventually they arrived at the monastery of Thyangboche. Coffee-coloured, its gold-plated roofs gleamed in the sun.

The first stage of the actual assault attempt

A terrifying crevasse is crossed by a makeshift bridge consisting of two ladders tied together

began in April when Hunt led a team to reconnoitre the Khumby glacier and icefall, seeking a route to the Western Cwm, an enclosed valley leading to the South Col, and from there to the summit. The going was difficult, the landscape a polar nightmare. Great blocks of ice of every conceivable shape were ground together as the glacier imperceptibly crept down the valley, every now and then groaning under the pressure. The climbers made their hazardous way past towering pinnacles of crumbling ice, some as tall as office blocks, which would eventually break away and come crashing to the floor of the valley. They inched across bottomless crevasses, forced open by the unbelievable pressures generated by the moving glacier. Sometimes they leapt the crevasses, at other times they had to cross flimsy ice bridges which often threatened to collapse under their weight. They also carried their own bridge consisting of two giant tree trunks which the Sherpas had manhandled all the way from the tree-line at 3,600 metres. They were now climbing at 5,400 metres. A number of the worst crevasses were named by the climbers, among them, Mike's Horror, Hillary's Horror and Hellfire Alley.

Camp II was established halfway up the icefall at 5,820 metres and then Camp III at the edge of the cwm. From these camps the climbers began their acclimatisation programme, tackling less difficult peaks, practising rope-work and making the way safe for the porters by securing fixed ropes to act as handrails. They improvised a bridge over a wide crevasse by fixing together two sections of an aluminium ladder. The Sherpas crawled across this flimsy structure, weighed down with their heavy loads without turning a hair.

Hillary and Tensing, climbing together for the first time, found a path to the centre of the Cwm where Camp IV was set up. During the first week in May, Camp V at 6,600 metres and Camp VI, at 6,700 metres were established on the face of the mountain Lhotse. The expedition made its way across this mountain to reach Everest. At these heights it was necessary to use oxygen, which, although it increased climbing efficiency, brought with it other problems. Every kilogram carried at high altitudes becomes a serious handicap and now the climbers were burdened down with heavy oxygen cylinders. Hunt began to plan the final assault. Lowe, Westmacott and Bond were to lead a group of Sherpa porters to establish Camp VII on the face of Everest. Noyce, Wylie and their Sherpas would carry on from there, and climb with supplies to establish Camp VIII on the South Col. At the first break in the weather Charles Evans and Tom Bourdillon would have a crack at the summit from the South Col; if they failed they would be replaced by Edmund Hillary and Tensing Norkay.

So on the morning of 28 May, Hillary and Tensing left Camp VIII to establish their final camp on the south ridge. Accompanied by Lowe, Alfred Gregory and Sherpa Ang Nymia, they carried between them over 127 kilos of oxygen and supplies, every item of which was vital to success. The going was painfully slow and they used up too much oxygen. At 8,400 metres they passed the shreds of the tent which Lambert and Tensing had abandoned the previous year and which marked the highest point in their attempt. At last they reached the sloping ledge which was to be the site for the assault camp. After handshakes and good wishes, Lowe, Gregory and Ang Nymia set off on their tedious return journey to the South Col, leaving Hillary and Tensing to pitch their tent in the gathering gloom.

After a miserable night, Hillary and Tensing dragged themselves from their sleeping bags at 4am on 29 May. Shivering in a temperature of −27°C they breakfasted, once again drinking vast quantities of highly sweetened lemon juice, and prepared to have a crack at the summit. Hillary's boots, which he had taken off because they were wet when he rolled into his sleeping bag now stood, stiff and frozen in the corner of the tent. As it took two hours to defreeze these over the cooker, it was 6.30am before they were ready to start. They had on string singlets, woollen underclothes, woollen shirts, woollen pullovers, thick down trousers and hooded jackets, several pairs of socks, windproof trousers and jackets and heavily spiked boots. On their hands they wore three pairs of gloves – silk, woollen and windproof. Tinted goggles guarded against snow-blindness, and they liberally smeared their faces with cream as a protection against frostbite. They heaved on their oxygen equipment, took up their ice-axes, and, lashed together with a strong nylon rope, moved out on to the snow slope leading to the summit. There was one blessing, the wind had dropped.

Fresh snow, not yet packed down, made the going slow and strenuous. At each step they sank up to their knees. They were using up too much energy and consequently too much oxygen. Unless they found firm going soon they would never make it. For half-an-hour they floundered on, conscious of the need to move quickly, but aware of the treacherous, crumbling surface lying beneath the deep layer of snow. To Hillary's horror part of the slope broke away from beneath his feet and went plummeting down a sheer drop of thousands of metres. 'It was a nasty shock,' he later wrote, 'my whole training told me that the slope was exceedingly dangerous, but at the same time I was saying to myself, "Ed, my boy, this is Everest – you've got to push it a bit harder."'

By 9am they had reached the South Summit and looked along the ridge to the main summit that had so daunted Evans and Bourdillon two days previously. The ridge was indeed a daunting sight. Steep and narrow, the rock beneath the coating of snow and ice had been eroded over the years into a brittle mass that could break away under the climber's feet at any time. A sheer fall of thousands of metres awaited a hasty step or stumble. Hillary decided that it was too dangerous to attempt the knife-edged ridge and made for a snow slope to the left of it.

If this proved to be solid-packed snow they had a chance. Their luck was in, the surface proved to be hard and was ideal for cutting steps. Slowly, but surely, a step at a time the two men hacked their way towards the top of the slope which reached halfway to the summit. Leading, Hillary would cut out a step while Tensing secured him with a tight rope in case he should slip. Then, belaying the rope round his ice-axe, firmly driven into the snow, he would in turn help Tensing up.

The ridge to the summit. The footsteps of the two climbers can just be seen on the left-hand side.
Inset: *Tensing on the summit carrying his ice-axe with many flags attached to it*

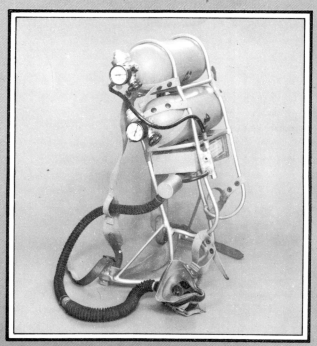

The oxygen equipment used by the climbers

the outlet valve. A few minutes more and Tensing, unable to exhale his carbon dioxide would have passed out and fallen into space taking Hillary with him. He quickly cleared the icicles from the Sherpa's mask and then examined his own. It too was badly iced up; he cleared it and they moved on again.

They reached the end of the snow slope and were confronted by a vertical wall of solid rock, too difficult to climb at an altitude of nearly 8,700 metres. Hillary searched for a way round it, but the only possible route meant climbing down 30 metres to the left, over flat slabs of rock slippery with ice, and then moving up again. This he rejected at once, as to go back would use up too much precious oxygen. As he looked over the surface of the vertical rock, Hillary caught sight of a pinnacle of ice which had moved away from the rock face making a chimney nearly 12 metres high. At some time it would break away completely and crash down. Now they were so close to the top the two men decided to risk climbing this chimney.

Hillary glanced back, and noticed that his companion was moving dangerously slowly and appeared to be in difficulties. Icicles hanging from his oxygen mask were blocking

Hillary wriggled himself into the gap between ice and rock, and feeling for holds with his hands, he braced his body to jam himself in

A view from the summit.

the chimney. Slowly, he wormed his way upwards. His spiked boots dug into the ice and gave him leverage. Anxiously Tensing watched his progress. Although he had Hillary tightly belayed, he knew that if the ice pinnacle broke away he would have no chance of holding his companion's plunging body as it hurtled past or of stopping himself being carried away with him. At last, gasping with the exertion, Hillary was able to grasp the rim of the chimney and lever himself painfully on to a rocky ledge. He rested for a short while to recover his breath, then helped Tensing to climb up the same way. By now both men were nearly exhausted, and before them lay a ridge which climbed sharply upwards away from them. They had no idea what lay beyond the top of the ridge. There might well be another vertical face similar to the one they had just climbed. Near to exhaustion as they were, this would probably spell defeat.

The slope appeared to be endless as slowly, wearily they moved on. Hillary later wrote: 'I asked Tensing to belay me strongly, and I started cutting a cautious line of steps up the ridge. Peering from side to side and thrusting with my ice-axe, I tried to discover a possible cornice, but everything seemed solid and firm. I waved Tensing up to me. A few more whacks of

Hillary, Hunt and Tensing with celebratory garlands after the news of their great achievement has been given to the world

the ice-axe, a few more weary steps, and we were on the summit of Everest.'

It was 11.30am on 29 May. At last, after more than thirty years of endeavour the legendary mountain had been conquered.

CHAPTER 10

Ordeal at the Foot of the World

*Dark, evil-looking figures,
some partly clothed in otter skins,
others almost naked, stood or squatted
outside their hovels, gazing
intently at the ship.*

Sir Francis Chichester was not the first man to sail round the world single-handed. Seventy years earlier, an American sea captain, Joshua Slocum, did it in the *Spray*. Whereas Chichester took less than nine months, Slocum's voyage lasted for almost three years, during which time he packed in more adventure than most men see in a lifetime.

Slocum, who came from a seafaring family, was the captain of one of the famous American clipper ships that could outsail most other ships of the day. People paid a high price for cargoes arriving in the fastest ships, and the American clipper captains raced each other to be the first with the China tea crop and the first to the gold fields of Australia and America. The ships themselves were sleek, beautiful craft, with sweeping rake and stern, whose hundreds of square metres of canvas called for the most complicated system of handling. Like his father Slocum was a born sailor and boat-builder.

'My father,' he once said, 'was the sort of man, who, if wrecked on a desert island, would find his way home, if he had a clasp knife and could find a tree.'

In the 1890s steam was taking over from sail and many captains of graceful sailing ships found themselves out of a job. Joshua Slocum, brought up on sail, knew nothing of steam and had no wish to learn. The smelly coal-fired steamers were not for him. It was a sailing ship or nothing. Out of work, he looked round for a ship of his own. A friend offered to give him the *Spray*, an old wreck of a sloop he owned.

'About as old as Noah's Ark', the locals said.

Undaunted, Slocum got to work and rebuilt her from the keel upwards, and at the end of a year he was the proud skipper-owner of an eminently seaworthy craft. While he was building the *Spray*, the idea of sailing round the world, grew in his mind, so he made her particularly sound and seaworthy. A miracle of speed she was ideally suited for single-handed sailing. She practically sailed herself.

In the autumn of 1895 he weighed anchor, sailing east across the Atlantic. He reached Gibraltar, and astonished everyone by stepping ashore very smartly dressed in formal sea-captain's uniform of blue frock coat, high stiff collar, black tie and waistcoat. The modest *Spray* might have been a fashionable 'Four-

master'. Slocum had planned to sail through the Suez Canal, but after an encounter with North African pirates, he changed his mind and sailed west, back across the Atlantic. He decided to sail round the world the other way, which meant rounding the fabled Cape Horn.

From the time of Magellan and Drake, Cape Horn had been regarded by mariners with superstitious dread. To catch sight of the legendary *Flying Dutchman*, doomed for ever to sail those waters, meant for certain that a vessel would be ship-wrecked. Its violent storms and mountainous seas made the area notorious amongst mariners. It was a place to be avoided by even the biggest and best-equipped ships, and for a man to attempt to round it single-handed was regarded as madness.

For 63 days and nights, Slocum battled his way round the Horn. Time and again he was blown back. At last the wind was in his favour

Slocum, stepping ashore in Gibraltar, impeccably dressed in a sea-captain's uniform. Inset: *Slocum towards the end of his life*

113

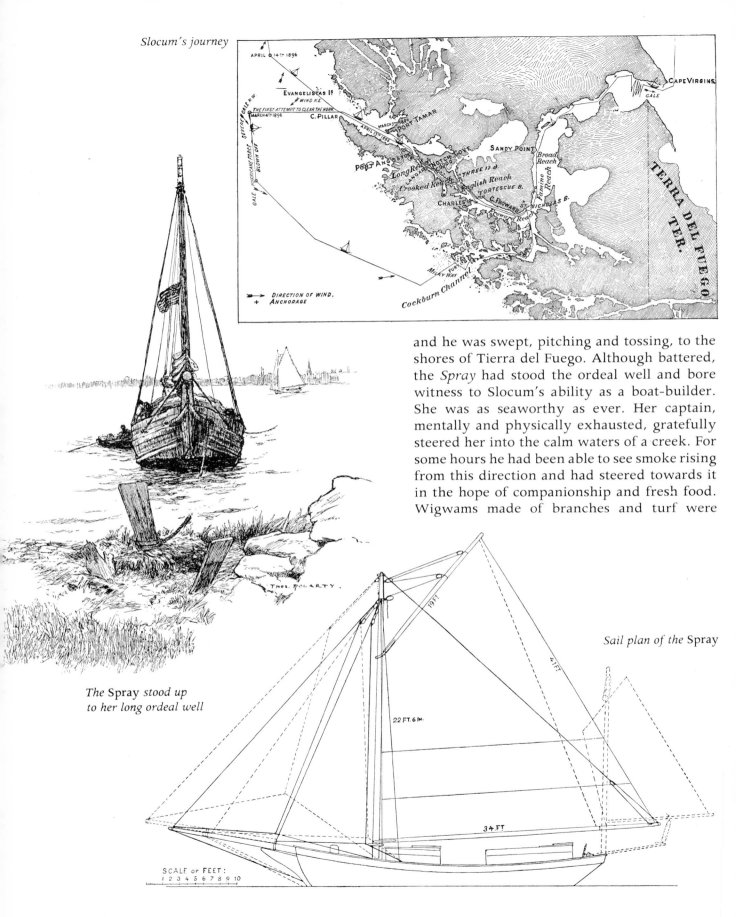

Slocum's journey

APRIL 14TH 1896

EVANGELISTAS I?
WIND N.E.
THE FIRST ATTEMPT TO CLEAR THE HORN
MARCH 4TH 1896
C. PILLAR

CAPE VIRGINS
GALE

PORT TAMAR

SANDY POINT

TERRA DEL FUEGO TER.

PORT ANGOSTO
Long Reach
Crooked Reach
English Reach
TORTESCUE B.
CHARLES I?
C. FROWARD

Broad Reach

DIRECTION OF WIND.
ANCHORAGE

Cockburn Channel

THOS. FOGARTY.

*The Spray stood up
to her long ordeal well*

and he was swept, pitching and tossing, to the shores of Tierra del Fuego. Although battered, the *Spray* had stood the ordeal well and bore witness to Slocum's ability as a boat-builder. She was as seaworthy as ever. Her captain, mentally and physically exhausted, gratefully steered her into the calm waters of a creek. For some hours he had been able to see smoke rising from this direction and had steered towards it in the hope of companionship and fresh food. Wigwams made of branches and turf were

Sail plan of the Spray

19 FT.
41 FT
22 FT. 6 IN.
34 FT

SCALE OF FEET:
1 2 3 4 5 6 7 8 9 10

114

scattered over the low ground near the shore, with smoke curling through holes in the roofs. From them wafted the stench of smoke, rancid butter and the refuse thrown outside. Dark, evil-looking figures, some partly clothed in otter skins, others almost naked, stood or squatted outside their hovels, gazing intently at the *Spray*. A raw wind blew down from the mountains, and snow lay in patches around the village. Slocum marvelled at the hardiness of the half-naked, Stone Age savages. They were a nomadic people, living on fish, mussels and sea urchins, supplemented by berries and edible plants. Stranded whales supplied them with a valuable source of oil, with which they covered themselves. It was a desperate struggle to survive and the Fuegans had little hesitation in stealing from anyone, as previous crews visiting the country had found to their cost.

Slocum had heard of their reputation, and realised that, alone and unprotected, he was an easy prey for the natives. They had only to creep aboard while he slept, batter him to death with their stone hatchets, and loot and dismantle his ship at their leisure. He was far too exhausted to continue his voyage without proper rest, and the *Spray* required some urgent repairs. He dragged himself on deck, eyes heavy with sleep, and made his preparations to repel any unwanted boarders. Then he went below and turned in. He was asleep as soon as his head hit the pillow.

In the early hours of the morning, he was awakened by a blood-curdling shriek. Leaping out of his bunk, he grabbed his rifle and dashed up the companionway. Half-a-dozen natives were leaping about, howling and clawing the air. Before turning in, Slocum had sprinkled the deck with carpet tacks, and as he later wrote: 'One cannot step on a tack without saying

A huge wave hits the Spray *off the Patagonian coast*

something about it.' At the sight of Slocum the Fuegans, 'jumped pell-mell: some into their canoes, some into the sea.' For good measure the lone sailor fired several rounds over their heads, 'to let the savages know I was at home, and then I turned in again.' The Fuegans did not try to molest him again.

After weeks of struggling against fierce gales and tempestuous seas, Slocum at last rounded the Horn and sailed into the Pacific. His leisurely cruise, took him amongst other places, to the island made famous by *Robinson Crusoe*, Fernandez Island. He then went on to Samoa and Australia. From there he sailed through the Indian Ocean, round the Cape of Good Hope and into the Atlantic. He crossed his outward track in May, 1898. He had sailed right round the world, single-handed, the first man ever to do so. He survived a tornado, and at last dropped anchor in Newport, in June, 1898, after a voyage of more than 73,600 kilometres.

In 1909. aged sixty-five, Joshua Slocum set off alone in the *Spray* to explore the Orinoco and the Amazon. He was never heard of again.

Slocum's chronometer

Slocum warning off the Fuegans

CHAPTER 11

Six Men against a Fleet

*He was anxious not to be
caught in a sea of fire, when the
surface mines exploded and ignited the oil,
so he struck out for the ship and
managed to scramble aboard.*

The periscope broke the surface and began to turn through a 180 degree arc as the submarine commander, Captain Count Julio Borghese, scanned the horizon for possible danger. The Italian submarine, *Scire*, had crossed from Leros in Greece on a secret mission; to sink the two remaining battleships of the British Mediterranean Fleet, HMS *Valiant* and HMS *Queen Elizabeth*. The night of 18 December 1941 found her 2.5 kilometres from Alexandria in Egypt which was the main British naval base in that area and a natural harbour virtually impregnable to attack. The operation had been carefully planned and rehearsed over many months, using a detailed model of the British base. Every precaution had been taken to keep the attempt secret and no hint of the attack had reached the British from their numerous agents in Italy, where the 'Small-Weapons Unit' had undergone training.

Borghese ordered *Scire* to surface, until the dirty off-shore water lapped over the submarine's narrow deck. Six Italian frogmen, led by their commander, Lieutenant-Captain Luigi de la Penne, made their way to the special torpedo hatch. The submarine went down until the frogmen, wearing protective rubber suits, were waist-deep in water. They dragged their 'chariots', two-men torpedoes, and made ready for the attack. These manned torpedoes, 'maiali' or 'pigs' as they were called by the frogmen, were 5.5 metres long with a diameter of half-a-metre and were propelled by two men sitting astride them. They were powered by an almost silent electric motor and could reach a top speed of 4 kilometres an hour. They had a range of 16 kilometres and a maximum working depth of 30 metres. The front section of the 'pig', which was the warhead, was detachable. It was 1.40 metres long, and contained about 300 kilograms of high explosive, more than enough to blow a sizeable hole in a large ship. The warhead was detached by releasing an airscrew, and it was then attached to its target by wire ropes magnetically clamped to the sides of the ship. The centre part of the torpedo was a gravity compensating tank, which allowed the 'pig' to submerge or surface. The frogmen sat behind a protective housing, and behind them were located the steering mechanism, the motor and a tool-box containing important equipment such as compressed air net-cutters, magnetic clamps and a compressed air net-lifter.

Luigi de la Penne ordered his men to mount their torpedoes; with him was Leading-Seaman Emilio Bianchi. Their job was to get rid of *Valiant*. The target for Captain Antonio Marceglia and Leading-Seaman Spartaco Schergat was *Queen Elizabeth*, and Captain Vincenzo Martelotta and Frogman-Sergeant Mario Marino were given an unknown aircraft-carrier as their target. In a hushed voice Captain Borghese wished them luck; he knew they

would need it. Sound travelled quickly over the still water so he closed the conning tower hatch carefully. At once *Scire* started to submerge. Borghese was anxious to be on his way home, although he was not looking forward to braving the 8 kilometres wide minefield that ringed Alexandria. There had been one or two nerve-wracking moments on the way over.

Left to themselves the frogmen made a last-minute inspection of their Davis Apparatus, a British invention, used mainly for escaping from stricken submarines. Although oxygen rebreathers were dangerous to use at 30 metres, the Italians had to wear them because the stream of bubbles left by standard scuba equipment would have made them conspicuous. The British, who had already suffered at the hands of Italian frogmen, were now very much aware of the danger and kept careful watch.

The Italian frogmen mounting their torpedoes
Inset: *Captain, later Commander, Junio Borghese*

The electric motors were started and the attack force headed towards Alexandria. The 'pigs' were submerged to the frogmen's eye level. Navigation was easy, for countless revolving searchlights which reached many kilometres out to sea, pin-pointed the harbour. The searchlights were of little danger to the frogmen as only the top of their heads were above water. It was 8 pm. The water was pitch-black and bitterly cold as they steered towards the three thick steel anti-submarine nets that guarded the entrance to the harbour. They were covering 4 kilometres an hour and this seemed painfully slow. They were very much aware of the patrolling guard-boat which occasionally dropped a random depth-charge. The fact that they were riding astride high-explosive torpedoes did nothing to allay their fears.

When at last they reached the submarine nets, they were already numbed with cold and hardly able to manoeuvre their 'chariots'. In the distance the guard-boat turned and headed in their direction. De la Penne signalled to dive. They went down into the murky water, searching for an opening in the nets. The protective housings parted the water in front of them. Frantically, de la Penne waved his arm: there were explosives suspended from the nets. Just in time they managed to swing the 'pigs' side-on. If they had hit one of the explosives the operation would have ended in a spectacular bang, as nearly 1,000 kilograms of high explosive went up. The thick steel netting called for compressed air cutters, but they realised that these made far too much noise, as British naval ratings were listening in on sound-detection equipment a few metres above them. There was nothing for it but to surface again and try to pass over the nets. But they found this impossible as the nets were too high in the water. They were shivering with cold as they wallowed about in the swell, wondering how they were to get into the harbour. Italian Naval Intelligence were unaware of the difficulty of penetrating the submarine nets despite the number of their agents in Alexandria. Luigi de la Penne was desperate, but then they had a stroke of luck. At midnight the lighthouse at the harbour entrance suddenly began to flash; the barriers opened and a troopship and three destroyers sailed into the harbour basin. The Italians followed them unnoticed under the surface, then they split up for the attack.

The torpedo sinks further and further into the black mud of the harbour bottom

De la Penne and Bianchi knew exactly where *Valiant* lay and made straight for her, passing by units of the French Fleet who were also based at Alexandria. A small light flashed aboard *Valiant* as a sailor lit a cigarette. Just short of the battleship they encountered a square of steel netting surrounding it. The two Italians struggled to drag their 'pig' over the netting and aimed it at the giant, black shadow looming ahead. In seconds the torpedo brushed against the side of the battleship, but de la Penne's hands were icy and stiff and he found it hard to cut the motor. At last he managed it and the torpedo remained leaning slightly against the side of *Valiant*. He tried to edge the 'pig' beneath the keel of the ship but it would not budge; something seemed to be holding it back. He signalled Bianchi to go and investigate. As he sat and waited for his colleague to return, the nose of the torpedo dipped and it began to sink rapidly. With a lurch it hit the bottom, settling into the thick mud. He revved the engine to full power but this only helped to drive the 'pig' deeper into the black, slimy ooze of the harbour bed. De la Penne climbed off and flashed his torch along the length of the torpedo. He saw that a steel cable had wound itself around the propeller, completely immobilising it. It was still too far from *Valiant* to do any significant damage. De la Penne later wrote: 'We had arrived a few metres from the target, after years of preparation and work, and now it had all come to an end.' He felt very much alone.

Bianchi had disappeared, probably because his oxygen rebreather had failed as they were so deep. His own breathing was difficult.

Somehow he must drag the 'pig' until it lay directly under the target. Desperately, up to his chest in mud, he heaved at the 5.5 metre torpedo. Slowly, bit by bit he dragged it towards *Valiant*. He had become weak and dizzy, but he was determined to succeed. He had only one thought in his mind, to get to the ship. At last the 'pig' was under the keel of the battleship, directly below an ammunition locker. He had made it. He released the warhead, set the fuse and covered the instruments with mud. He fought his way to the surface almost blacking out, only to be met with a hail of bullets. Alerted when the 'pig' had hit the side of *Valiant*, her crew were now lining the rail firing at the Italian. The frogman, swimming as he had never swum before, reached the battleship's mooring buoy and clambered on to it. He was surprised and delighted to find Bianchi already crouching there. Soon a ship's cutter pulled alongside and the Italians were bundled aboard with scant ceremony and taken onto their target. De la Penne, interrogated by *Valiant*'s commander, Captain Charles Morgan, refused to say where he had planted the warhead. The two men were imprisoned, to their horror, in the ammunition locker directly above the fused explosive charge. Both the Italian frogmen and the British sailors who guarded them were pale and nervous. The Italians were only too well aware of a time mechanism ticking away below them.

Meanwhile Marceglia and Schergat had found little difficulty in locating *Queen Elizabeth*, which lay about 300 metres from *Valiant*. They dived under the battleship's protective net and manoeuvred their torpedo under her hull. Within minutes they had released the warhead, attached it with magnetic clamps and fused it. Recklessly, they surfaced their 'chariot' almost alongside their target, and were lucky to make off unseen. Italian Naval Intelligence had told them of a deserted quay in the ancient trading port of Alexandria where they would be able to land unseen. They slipped along at eye-level depth in the direction of Alexandria, threading their way through anchored ships. On the way they scattered the

surface of the water with small explosive charges which would ignite any leaking oil from *Queen Elizabeth* when she blew up. As they neared the shore they sank the 'pig' which was fitted with a self-destruction mechanism. After eight hours in the water, they were tired and shivering, but elated that they had completed a highly dangerous mission which many of their senior officers had secretly thought impossible. They crawled ashore and quickly struggled out of their rubber suits which they hid along with their other equipment. They managed to leave the dockyard and set off for Rosetta at the mouth of the Nile, where they were to rendezvous with an Italian submarine the next day.

The third team, Martelotta and Marino, had been unable to fulfil their allotted mission, as the aircraft carrier had sailed 24 hours earlier for the Pacific. They determined to find a suitable target and searched until they located a 7,750 tonne naval tanker, *Sagona*. They left their 300 kilograms of explosive dangling below *Sagona*'s stern and set off astride their 'chariot' for the quay where Marceglia and Schergat had already landed, scattering their surface charges as they went. But by this time the alarm had been sounded and ships throughout the harbour were weighing anchor and making for the open sea. When they struggled ashore at the old port they were met by a British naval patrol who promptly arrested them and

The two Italians, having successfully accomplished their mission, wait on the buoy to be picked up by the enemy
Inset: *Captain Luigi de la Penne*

whisked them off to Naval Intelligence head-quarters for questioning. By then it was 6am and the charges were set to go off at 6.05am; it was now too late for the British to take effective defensive measures.

In the ammunition locker aboard *Valiant* nerves were stretched to breaking point and conversation had long since ceased. There were only twenty minutes to go when de la Penne requested an interview with the ship's captain.

'They brought me to him', he wrote, 'and I told him that there was no hope now, that the ship would explode, and if he wished he could bring the crew to safety.' But the captain refused to co-operate until the Italian had told him where he had placed the charge. De la Penne was frightened, but defiant, and refused

to say. He was led back to the ammunition locker. However, now he was completely alone, for the British sailors and Bianchi were no longer there. Captain Morgan had obviously anticipated his advice and abandoned ship. There was only a skeleton crew above decks. In an agony of suspense de la Penne waited for the explosion, through the long, dragging minutes, fighting to control his nerves. He says: 'Then, at the moment when I was still calculating that the charge should explode at any time, I felt an explosion, or rather the beginning of one. Then I found myself in the water, recovering consciousness.'

Valiant had split open and was listing badly. The Italian looked towards *Queen Elizabeth*, silhouetted against the rising sun. There was a sudden flash then the noise of the explosion hit him. A great column of oil gushed from the funnel of the stricken ship, spreading over the water about the frogman. He was anxious not to be caught in a sea of fire when the surface mines exploded and ignited the oil, so he struck out for *Valiant* and managed to scramble aboard. The upper deck was a scene of chaos as seamen dashed about attempting to lower the ship's boats. Both battleships were out of commission for months. *Valiant* had to be dragged to dry dock and *Queen Elizabeth* lay with a 12 metre hole in her hull. The Mediterranean Fleet had been reduced to a cruiser squadron and a few destroyers, thanks to six brave men.

Next day the Italian submarine waited in vain opposite Rosetta for the frogmen. Marceglia and Schergat had been picked up near the rendezvous point, victims of their own naval intelligence, who had given them British banknotes which were not valid in Egypt.

De la Penne swimming in the oil covered water after Valiant *has exploded*

CHAPTER 12

Sergeant Ward VC

*Half-out, one leg hanging
in space, he was hit by the fierce
slipstream and all but torn away
from the aircraft.*

Münster sprawled below them, spitting and crackling like an enormous firework display. Wave after wave of Wellingtons had emptied their bomb loads on the already devastated industrial town. Lately, both sides had intensified their raids on key industrial targets, plastering them with high explosives night after night. By concentrating their attacks on armament works, aircraft factories and heavy industrial and chemical plants, they hoped to stem the output of war material and cripple the economy of the enemy. Anti-aircraft defences were strengthened to counteract these attacks. Vital industrial plant was ringed by countless batteries of anti-aircraft guns which threw up an enormous amount of 'flack'. In 1941 British airmen were finding that an increasing number of night-fighters, the fearsome Messerschmitt

110's, were coming up to meet them. This was an added danger they found difficult either to elude or fight off. The Germans dived on them out of the darkness at over 560kph. They were small, half-seen shadows spitting cannon shells and tracer and were on them before they could swing their machine-gun turrets to bear on such elusive fast-moving targets.

Sergeant Ward gazed down through the side window of the Wellington and saw their own stick of bombs land. There was a line of flashes, 'one, two, three, four', then the bomber was flung sideways as if thrown by a giant hand. White streams of 40mm tracer shells rushed up to meet them. They were flying in towards the end of the raid and the flack batteries had settled into the range. Their mission completed, Squadron Leader Widdowson, the pilot, hastily

During 1941, both the British and the Germans made many crippling raids over enemy cities and towns

banked the heavy bomber and thankfully headed for home. 'It had been a piece of cake', he thought, 'hardly any flack and as yet no sign of Luftwaffe night-fighters.' Widdowson, an experienced pilot, was a born leader who slipped easily into the friendly but disciplined atmosphere of Bomber Command. He was reliable rather than spectacular, and had the complete confidence of his crew.

Sergeant James Allen Ward, who came from Wangamu in New Zealand, had been Widdowson's second pilot for some time, and the two men understood each other perfectly. They made a good team each having complete faith in the other. Like the skipper, Ward had a string of bombing missions behind him. Two Kiels, one Düsseldorf, one Cologne, one Brest, one Münster, one Mannheim and now, on 7 July 1941, another Münster. An old hand, he too thought tonight's mission had been easy, almost uneventful. The flack had been nowhere near as heavy as one time at Düsseldorf.

The Wellington was roaring through the beautiful moonlit night 3,900 metres above the Zuider Zee. Ahead lay the North Sea and home. In the bitter cold of the cockpit, all the hot coffee had gone. Ward's mind turned to the breakfast waiting for them back at base. After a quick de-briefing, a shower and a leisurely breakfast he would have the whole day free before him. Busily he began to plan.

There was a sudden crackle over the intercom followed by the voice of Sergeant Allen Box, the rear gunner. '110! 110!' Cannon shells and bullets raked the Wellington from stem to stern. The night-fighter had zoomed at them from below, viciously opening up at point-blank range. The bomber's guns began to chatter as the German came in for a second run. Grimly hanging on to his guns, Box swung his turret to follow the 110, but the damage had been done. The front gunner had been hit, and the hydraulic system put out of action so that the bomb doors fell open. The cockpit was rapidly filling with smoke and fumes. It was impossible to estimate the extent of the damage, but if the hydraulic system was out of action they were in very serious trouble. The gun turrets, their only defence, were operated electrically and if the undercarriage could not be cranked down by

hand and locked, it would mean a dicey belly-landing with neither air brakes nor flaps and they would be coming in at over 160kph.

'Skipper to crew. Report damage!'

There was no reply. The radio and intercom sets were dead. The engine note had changed to a complaining whine, but still throbbed on. The navigator put his head round the cockpit door with the news that the starboard engine had been badly hit and it was spluttering and spraying petrol all over the wing. If the engine were to cut completely they would have to bale out, and take their chances in the cold grey waters of the Zuider Zee.

The Messerschmitt came in again. Tracer bullets flickered across the nose of the Wellington. Widdowson took the aircraft into a dive. Had he thought tonight was a piece of cake? The Messerschmitt 110 sheared off, making for base. It was soon obvious why.

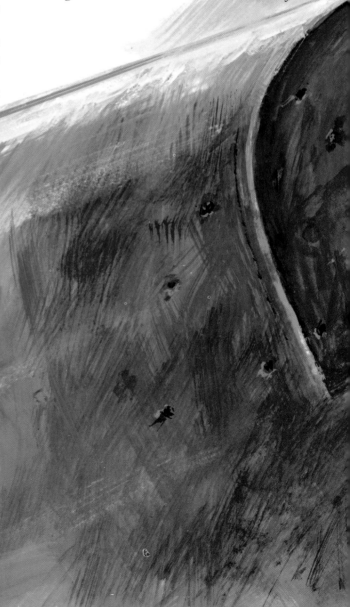

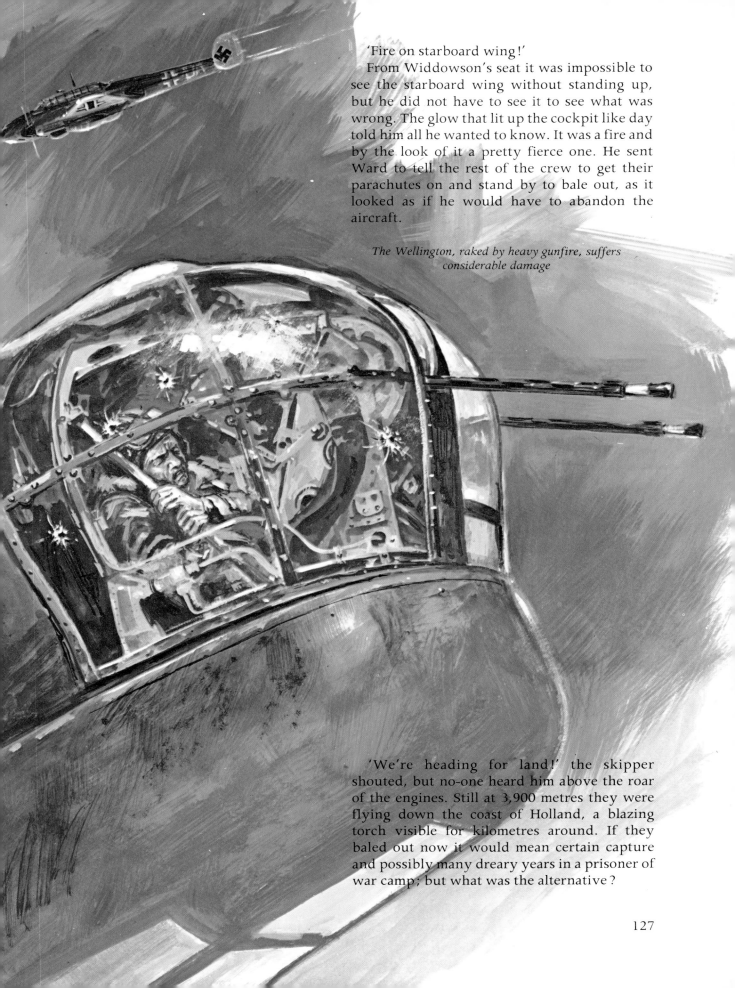

'Fire on starboard wing!'

From Widdowson's seat it was impossible to see the starboard wing without standing up, but he did not have to see it to see what was wrong. The glow that lit up the cockpit like day told him all he wanted to know. It was a fire and by the look of it a pretty fierce one. He sent Ward to tell the rest of the crew to get their parachutes on and stand by to bale out, as it looked as if he would have to abandon the aircraft.

The Wellington, raked by heavy gunfire, suffers considerable damage

'We're heading for land!' the skipper shouted, but no-one heard him above the roar of the engines. Still at 3,900 metres they were flying down the coast of Holland, a blazing torch visible for kilometres around. If they baled out now it would mean certain capture and possibly many dreary years in a prisoner of war camp; but what was the alternative?

127

Widdowson might be able, with a great deal of luck, to crash-land his kite in one of the low-lying Dutch fields. But this part of the coast, which was directly in the line of the RAF bomber routes, would sure to be littered with concrete obstacles. The third alternative was to try to make it back to base across the North Sea. If they failed to reach the English coast it would mean baling out over the sea with the danger of floating helplessly hoping to be picked up by an Air Sea Rescue patrol. He was the skipper responsible for the lives of his crew, and he, and he alone, would have to make the decision.

Back in the fuselage of the bomber, Ward was organising the fire-fighting, but with little success. The fire extinguishers were proving useless. Even by hanging from the astro-hatch at full stretch the foam was not reaching the fire as it was too far along the wing. Flames from the rear of the starboard engine were being whipped away into the darkness astern by the slipstream. This proved to be a blessing. Although the crew could see it was hopeless,

they still kept trying to put out the fire. One of the crew even attempted to douse the flames with the coffee remaining in his thermos.

Then Ward realised that the fire was not gaining on the initial flare-up. The slipstream was carrying the flames astern, preventing them spreading along the wing. He hurried to the cockpit to report to the squadron leader. This information decided Widdowson to chance it back to the English coast. It was worth the risk when the alternative was possibly years in a German stalag. All his attention

Ward, hanging from the astro-hatch at full stretch is still unable to reach the consuming fire

was concentrated on keeping the Wellington airborne and somehow making England. He knew he could safely leave the New Zealander to cope with the fire.

They were well over the choppy waters of the North Sea when the fuel pipe split. Ward, watching the fire, noticed a sudden flare-up that turned into a roaring inferno, as petrol from the split pipe fed the flames. In a short time the whole aircraft would be ablaze. One glance at the sea below decided Ward; someone had to crawl out along the wing and somehow smother the flames. By now Widdowson had taken the Wellington down to 144kph, but they were still 4 kilometres up.

In a split second Ward made up his mind; it was up to him to put out the fire. But he must do it quickly; it would not do to think about it. He searched round until he found a canvas cockpit cover, serving as a cushion. That might be the very thing with which to smother the flames. He examined the astro-hatch. It would be a tight squeeze, and he would need to move as freely as possible once he was out on the wing, so, to the horror of the rest of the crew, he began to struggle out of his parachute. Finally, he was persuaded to keep it on, and helped by the navigator he clambered up to the astro-hatch.

Gingerly he stuck his head out, to be met with a blast of icy wind that snatched his breath away and stung his face. This was going to be impossible. A rope from the aircraft's rubber dinghy tied securely round his waist was held taut by the navigator. But Ward realised that the rope was more of a hindrance than a help. Quickly he put out of his mind the picture of himself dangling at the end of a rope, 4 kilometres up, from an aircraft travelling at 144kph. Now or never. The navigator gave the thumbs up sign and he eased himself through the astro-hatch. Half-out, one leg hanging in space, he was hit by the fierce slipstream and all but torn away from the aircraft and thrown into space. Even at 144kph the wind pressure was an awesome experience.

Slowly he edged himself out. His knuckles gleamed as he clung fiercely to the edge of the hatch and tried to flatten himself against the side of the aircraft. For a time he hung there in space while he worked out what he was going to do. The more he thought about his task, the less

129

feasible it became; he must be mad. Another few seconds and he would crawl back in and no one would blame him. He had to act immediately. Still clinging to the side of the hatch, his face centimetres from that of the anxious navigator, he began to kick a hole in the side of the fuselage to expose the framework and give himself a foothold. He lowered himself a little further, feeling for the foothold like a mountaineer crawling down a rock-face. But no mountaineer had ever experienced this roaring hell. He kicked-in another hole, and then further down, another. He was now at full stretch, and his arms felt as if they were being torn from their sockets and his hands and face were numb. Ward's groping foot at last touched the wing. He levered himself sideways against the slipstream and reached down with one hand, gripping a section of framework where the wing-covering had been stripped by the Messerschmitt's cannon shells. He crouched with both feet on the wing-root, and studied the surface between himself and the engine, which luckily had been fairly stripped exposing much of the framework. The flames were casting deep shadows that danced grotesquely across the wing, and it was bitterly cold. He let go his grip on the fuselage and threw himself full-length grabbing at the exposed framework with his free hand. Ward's legs slid sideways into space as the wind tore at them. He hung on for dear life and dragged his body sideways until his feet were well dug in. Shaking with effort and nervous strain, he lay there, buffeted

cockpit cover from under his flying jacket and began to push it down into the hole in the wing to block the leaking pipe, aware that at any second he might be blown off. At last, hanging on with his left hand, he stuffed the cover through the hole and managed to wedge it against the pipe, but the wind pressure blew it out again. In a flash, the cover was gone, but not before it had nearly dragged him from his precarious hold as he made a grab for it. Petrol was still being pumped out of the split fuel pipe, so Ward had achieved nothing. His only hope was to stop the flames spreading, so he tore away the wing fabric surrounding his side of the engine. Gradually it came away until the flaming petrol was only falling on bare metal. After tearing off all the fabric near the fire there was nothing to do but to get back inside. He was now pretty well all in. The journey back to the fuselage was a nightmare and once or twice he was convinced that he would never make it. The navigator had pulled the rope taut taking as much of the strain as he could. At last he reached the fuselage and by a super-human effort raised himself up and grabbed the edge of the astro-hatch. Willing hands dragged him into the Wellington, where he sank to the floor completely exhausted.

by the full force of the wind-pressure whipping across the top surface of the wing. 'It was like being in a terrific gale,' he later said, 'only much worse than any gale I've ever known.'

Once or twice he thought he was going to fall. Spreadeagled, he was prevented by his parachute from getting close to the wing and the wind kept lifting him up. Hastily he pulled the

The damaged Wellington making a successful crash-landing, thanks largely to the courage of Sergeant Ward

Although the fire had not been stopped, Ward had stopped it from spreading by tearing away the surrounding fabric. In due course it burned itself out. Widdowson flew the bomber across the North Sea without further trouble. When only a few kilometres from the airfield some of the petrol that had collected in the wing suddenly flared up, but this luckily died out almost immediately. The skipper's main concern now, was to bring the crippled Wellington safely down. With the hydraulics out of action he would have to land without flaps or wheel brakes, but fortunately the undercarriage could be pumped down manually and locked by means of the emergency system.

As he circled the airfield, coming in to land, he could see the emergency crews scuttling across the runway. They had spotted the open bomb doors. He was coming in too fast. The ground rushed up. There was a bump, and the plane tore along the runway towards the perimeter. It was doing about 48kph when it ploughed through the barbed wire at the end of the runway, then ground to a halt. They were safely down.

'Sergeant Ward seemed to take what he had done as a matter of course,' Widdowson said later, 'but in my opinion it was a wonderful show.' The Air Ministry thought the same and James Ward received the Victoria Cross.

CHAPTER 13

Notorious Colonel Blood

*The Captain soon managed
to catch up with the clergyman
and called upon him to yield. The desperate
robber whipped out a pistol and fired,
but the ball whined harmlessly
over his head.*

The Keeper of the Regalia, Edwards, was an old soldier, and he was enjoying himself. There had been more visitors than usual so far that day and already his tips were beginning to mount up. Even in 1670, visitors flocked to the Tower of London. They filed through its chambers filled with curious weapons and armour, staring at the spot where Queen Anne Boleyn had been executed or catching their breath at the sight of the rack and other gruesome relics in the torture chambers. But in those days torture had not long been abolished, which sent an extra tingle of fear up the spine of the visitor, and in the seventeenth century, the grim Norman fortress was still the principal prison for political prisoners. Visitors might also catch a glimpse of one of the many traitors who had conspired against the king, Charles II.

During the Restoration there was a steady stream of plots against the Crown. Earnest and vindictive men, Baptists, Quakers, Presbyterians, Congregationalists and Unitarians gathered in secret, conspiring to bring down the king and restore the rule of 'King Jesus'. Emissaries made their way by night along lonely roads, stealing from village to village. Informers, counter-informers and spies haunted the taverns and coffee houses of the City. It was more than a man's life was worth to speak out against the king in public; only among friends could he mutter his grievances, and even that was often dangerous. Everywhere weapons were gathered and men enlisted against the great day, the new Armageddon, when the ungodly king would be swept aside to be replaced by a new Commonwealth.

One of the leading conspirators was an Irishman, a self-styled colonel, Thomas Blood. At the outbreak of the Civil War he had been a trooper in 'Rupert's Horse'. Years later the Prince remembered him as a 'bold and dashing soldier'. When the tide began to turn against the Royalist cause, Blood defected to the Parliamentarians, becoming a lieutenant in Cromwell's New Army. After the Restoration his new-found fortune in land, given to him by the Commonwealth, was taken from him. Embittered by this treatment, he joined a conspiracy to take over Dublin Castle and sieze the Lord Lieutenant of Ireland, the Duke of Ormond. Inevitably an informer came forward and betrayed the plot. The conspirators were

taken to be executed, imprisoned or transported. Colonel Blood, however, escaped and was outlawed. From then on he flitted from plot to plot, and although each plot in turn failed, Blood always managed to get away in the nick of time. By 1670 he had set himself up as a physician and was living quietly in the little village of Romford, in Surrey, under the name of Allen.

Among Edwards's visitors to the Tower was a clergyman, his wife and nephew. They were up from the country and were eager to see everything. The clergyman, 'exceeding pleasant and jocose – a tall rough-boned man, with small legs, a pok-frecken face with little hollow blue eyes', was particularly interested in the

Royal Regalia, consisting of the crown, sceptre and orb. He judged the crown itself to be worth £100,000 but in fact the whole Regalia had only cost £6,000. Suddenly, the woman began to tremble. Within seconds she was shaken by violent convulsions. Her husband and Edwards, alarmed at her condition, tried to revive her as she lay writhing on the floor, but without success. Between them they carried her to Edwards's apartments, where his wife and daughter administered cordials and restoratives until the lady recovered. The clergyman was deeply grateful and obviously very much

The Tower in Stuart times, from an etching by Wenceslaus Hollar, the Anglo-Czech engraver

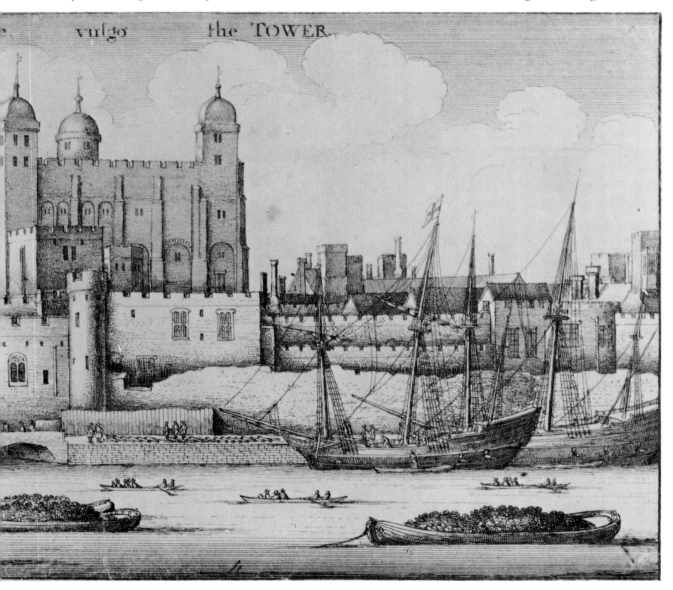

St. Edward's Crown, made for the coronation of King Charles II in 1661

relieved, and rewarded Edwards handsomely for his attention. Indeed, all three were profuse in their expressions of gratitude towards the keeper and his family. This incident led to an acquaintance between the two families which rapidly ripened into friendship. Edwards was flattered by the attention paid to him by a member of the church, and was only too willing to foster the friendship. Frequent visits made by the clergyman and his nephew invariably led to further meetings with the family.

A friendship between the two families begins after Edward's wife and daughter care for the clergyman's wife

The nephew, who was young and dashing, set out to charm the keeper's daughter. Soon the simple girl was infatuated with the handsome young man. The growing mutual attraction was watched benignly by the uncle, while the proud father and mother did everything in their power to throw the young couple together. They considered the nephew of a

Colonel Blood was a notorious plotter and opportunist who somehow always managed to extricate himself from his difficulties

clergyman to be a fine match, and were delighted to give their blessing, when some months later the nephew proposed marriage and their blushing daughter accepted. The clergyman insisted on making all the arrangements, and naturally insisted on marrying the couple himself. On 9 May 1671, the clergyman, his nephew and a friend, accompanied by two servants, rode to the Tower at about seven in the morning to make the final arrangements. Mrs Edwards, caught unprepared, was not ready to meet her guests at such an early hour and insisted on making herself presentable.

While they were chatting in the parlour it emerged that the friend had never seen the Regalia. Immediately the clergyman suggested that it would help to pass the time if Edwards were to show it to him. Anxious to please, the keeper led the way up the twisting stone steps to the room where the treasures were kept. As he opened the cupboard to take out the Regalia he was seized from behind and a cloak thrown over his head. He struggled frantically although half-choked by the cloak, but the men were too strong for him. He was soon bound, gagged, and for good measure, struck on the head with a mallet. But still his muffled cries could be heard from beneath the cloak, and either the clergyman or his friend – it has never been determined which – brutally drove a dagger into him. Although only slightly wounded, Edwards thought it prudent to lie still. He had no doubts that the ruthless men would not hesitate to stab him again, and the second time could prove fatal.

The clergyman grabbed the crown, bending it so that it would fit, unseen, under his cloak. The other man had slipped the orb into his baggy breeches and was busily trying to file the sceptre in two, so that it might be more easily hidden. They were suddenly startled by a warning shout from the nephew who was standing guard at the bottom of the stairs. Quickly they rushed down, and, pushing aside two young soldiers who stared at them in amazement, the three robbers ran off towards the Tower Gate. By a strange coincidence, Edwards's son, Talbot, who had been away at the continental wars, picked this very moment to return home with a friend, Captain Beckman. It was they who interrupted the robbers. Hearing the commotion below, Edwards wriggled free of his bonds, tore off the gag and shouting, 'treason and murder', staggered down the stairs.

In no time his son and Beckman were after the robbers. They brandished their pistols and raced towards the Tower Gate, just in time to see the villains disappearing into the crowds on Tower Hill. The soldiers cried: 'Treason! The crown is stolen!', but the wily clergyman added to the confusion by shouting, 'stop thief! stop thief!' Passers-by thought the two men were part of the chase, and allowed them through. Captain Beckman, a young man, soon managed to catch up with the clergyman and called upon him to yield. The desperate robber whipped out a pistol and fired, but the ball whined harmlessly over Beckman's head. An instant later the two men were rolling about the

Blood's daring attempt to steal the crown was nearly successful

Blood and his Accomplices
Escaping after stealing the CROWN from the TOWER.

The robbers are quickly captured and taken back to the Tower for identification

garbage-littered street in a 'robustious struggle', as they wrestled for possession of the crown. The clergyman broke free and drew a second pistol and fired again, but once again his shot flew wide. By now the Tower guards and young Edwards had arrived on the scene and the clergyman and his friend were easily overpowered. The nephew, mounted on his horse would have got away, if he had not ridden straight into a projecting cart pole. He lay on the cobbles, badly winded, and was taken by the guards without a struggle. The two servants, waiting with the horses outside the gate, were quick to make their escape at the first hint of trouble.

140

The robbers were dragged back to the Tower, where they were immediately identified by one of the warders. The clergyman, to the astonishment of his captors, was found to be none other than the notorious Colonel Blood. The so-called 'nephew' was his son, and the friend was an Anabaptist silk dyer, a known conspirator, named Parret. Warrants were quickly made out for their imprisonment. Blood was charged with, 'outlawry for treason and other great and heinous crimes in England'. Young Blood and Parret for 'dangerous crimes and practises'.

The most curious part of this exploit was to follow. As an outlawed traitor, caught red-handed in the act of stealing the crown, there could be only one possible outcome for Blood; a trip to Tyburn and an ignominious death at the end of a rope. Blood's attempt to steal the Regalia was regarded as more than mere robbery, particularly as the Chancellor's house had also recently been burgled and nothing stolen but the great seal of England. Rumours flew round the capital. Was the robbery a prelude to the assassination of the king and recognition of a usurper who hoped to strengthen his position by the possession of the crown and great seal? It was even hinted that Charles II, short of money as usual, had himself prompted Blood to steal the Regalia to sell.

The proceedings in Blood's case excited extraordinary interest throughout the country. Interest was not lessened by the unusual circumstances surrounding the crime. The Colonel and his fellow prisoners were first brought for questioning before the Provost-Marshal, Sir Gilbert Talbot. None of the three men would reveal their motives, accomplices, or the ultimate purpose of the exploit. In addition, Blood had the effrontery to demand an audience with the king. His bold request was granted to the astonishment of everyone, and three days later, on 12 May, he was summoned to Whitehall to appear before the king, his brother James, Duke of York and a few selected members of the Royal Household.

No record of that extraordinary interview has yet been discovered, and no satisfactory explanation put forward. After the interview Blood was returned to the Tower and in the following weeks, the gossips in the coffee shops talked of nothing else. All London looked forward to a day's holiday when the most no-

torious criminal of the time made the journey to Tyburn. But one man, the Duke of Ormond, doubted the outcome. As he hinted darkly to a friend: 'The man need not despair. Surely no king would wish to see a malefactor but with intention to pardon him.' He was about the only person to express his doubts and in the event he was proved right. Two months later a grant of pardon was issued to Colonel Thomas Blood, for, 'all the treasons, murders, felonies etc., committed by him alone or with others from the day of His Majesty's accession, 29 May 1660, to the present'. An incredulous nation could hardly believe it. They were further bewildered not long afterwards when Blood had his estates restored to him and was given a place at Court together with a pension of £500 a year in Irish lands.

No one has ever solved this mystery, but perhaps the clue lies somewhere in this letter which Blood wrote to the King from the Tower.

Blood has an audience with King Charles. The true facts of his pardon and release have never been discovered

'19 May 1671. Tower.
Colonel Blood to the king.

May it please your Majesty these may tell and inform you that Sir Thomas Osborne and Sir Thomas Littleton, both your treasurers for your Navy, that set me to steal your crown, but he that feed me with money was James Littleton Esq. 'Tis he that pays under your treasurer at the Pay Office. He is a very bold villainous fellow, a very rogue, for I and my companions have had money to encourage us upon this attempt. I pray no words of this confession, but I know your friends. Not else but am your Majesty's prisoner and if life spared your dutiful subject whose name is Blood, which I hope is not that your Majesty seeks after.'

CHAPTER 14

Buried Alive

*His legs were completely dead
and he was ravenously hungry, but he was
able to quench his thirst by sucking
handfuls of snow.*

Gerhard Freissegger awoke with a start. The hollow moan of the wind had changed to a frenzied roar as it flung itself at the small wooden hut. From his bunk he could see the snow being driven horizontally past the window. He had been in many storms, but in all his years in the mountains Freissegger had never seen one as bad as this. It was not a night to be outside. He looked round the warm, comfortable living room and thought that the company certainly did their employees proud.

In January 1951, the company was building a dam, high up on the side of the Sattelalp, for a new hydro-electric scheme at Heiligenblut in Austria. A two-stage cable car had been constructed to transport stores and materials up from the valley, hundreds of metres below. Freissegger was one of a team of three who manned the middle station. It was a seven day a week job, and they took it in turns to have a free weekend every three weeks. This Saturday it had been Freissegger's turn, but he had allowed one of his colleagues, who was married, to go in his place.

All day he and his other colleague, Siegfried Lindner, had been working at the station, supervising load after load of materials coming up from the valley. The weather was miserable. For several days now, snow had fallen continuously from a dark, leaden sky, blanketing the mountain in a heavy layer. As the afternoon wore on, Freissegger noticed that the wind was getting up. It looked like being a stormy night.

Freissegger and Lindner trudging home up the mountain after a hard day's work

'That's the last load for today,' called Lindner. By now it was quite dark and the wind had reached gale force. The two men closed down the station, put on their heavy top-coats and prepared to set out for their small three-roomed living hut, 45 metres uphill. They trudged homewards hit by the full blast of the wind, sinking up to their knees in the thick carpet of soft snow. By the time they had covered the distance to the hut they were shivering with cold, their faces tingling from the force of the driven snow.

'This is going to be a bad one!' said Freissegger. Lindner did not reply. He was too busy clearing the snow away from the bottom of the door, his mind on the hot meal ahead of them. In no time at all the stove had made the living room warm, and the two men, having eaten well, settled down to a comfortable evening, heedless of the moan of the wind outside. They were about to go to bed when the telephone began to rung. Lindner picked up the receiver.

'Winkelstation? Yes. Avalanche danger. Never mind, Gerhard and I'll come up and dig the two of you out in the morning if anything happens,' Lindner joked.

Winkelstation, the station higher up the Sattelalp, had received an urgent avalanche warning and they were naturally concerned. Freissegger and Lindner went to bed, confident that if there was an avalanche, it was more likely that Winkelstation would be hit and not them. Freissegger's room was bitterly cold so he decided to sleep in the warm living room, using the bunk normally occupied by his married colleague. It had been a tiring day, and he soon drifted off to sleep, faintly conscious of the fact that the wind had increased in strength.

He was now wide awake. He looked at the clock and saw that it was 2am.

'Just listen to that wind, Gerhard,' Lindner called from the next room. Before he could reply there was a splintering crash, an icy blast and the room seemed to fall in on him. It was suddenly pitch black and he couldn't see. Frantically, he cleared the snow away from his face, thankful that he could still breathe freely. For some seconds he lay there, dazed. The awful realization came to him that they had been hit by an avalanche. He struggled to free himself but to his horror was unable to move his left arm and his legs felt dead. Packed snow held him in a vice-like grip, rigidly pinning him to the bunk. He would have suffocated, had it not been for a roof beam that had fallen across his chest, keeping the snow off his his face.

'Siegfried,' he cried.

'Help me, Gerhard. Help me.'

So Lindner was still alive, but his voice sounded faint probably due to the pressure of the snow. There must be hundreds of tonnes of it above them. Panic-stricken he tore at it with his free hand but after a few minutes fell back, panting.

'Help me, Gerhard.'

Lindner's voice was definitely weaker now. Freissegger lay still.

'Don't worry, Siegfried,' he called, 'it's best to lie still and wait to be rescued. They'll be

here at first light.' He wondered if they would be able to stand the cold that long, then realised that it was not all that cold, as the snow pressing down on the blankets was insulating him. For some time the two men continued to call out to each other, but Lindner's voice had become very faint indeed.

Freissegger is trapped by the avalanche in his bed in the hut

'Siegfried,' he called. There was no answer. 'Siegfried.' Still no answer. Suddenly it was deathly quiet. He listened intently, but there was no sound of breathing. Lindner must be dead. He was alone. As this shattering fact hit him, he began to shout, panic surging up inside him. He forced himself to lie still. It could only be a matter of an hour or two before the rescue party arrived.

He heard voices and knew that a rescue team had arrived. He could hear them walking about above him and probing the snow with their spades as they searched for the hut. But the sound was very faint through the metres of snow above him.

The fairy tale village of Heiligenblut in Austria. Freissegger and Lindner were employees of a company building a dam, part of a hydro-electric scheme, to serve the village

148

He began to call and shout. 'Help. Help.'

The rescue team continued to move about. Sometimes he could hear their voices clearly, while at other times they were indistinct. They seemed to be having difficulty in finding the hut. Finally the sounds disappeared altogether. Perhaps they had only gone for digging equipment? It seemed an age to Freissegger before he heard them again. He began to shout frantically, over and over again, until he was hoarse. At the back of his mind was an awful dread. Although he continued to shout, he knew from bitter experience that quite often an avalanche victim can hear people above, but they cannot hear him, as sounds are deadened by tightly-packed snow.

For three days the rescuers combed the area, while Freissegger lay trapped below, in a frenzy of alternate hope and despair. His legs were completely dead and he was ravenously hungry, but he was able to quench his thirst by sucking handfuls of snow.

The rescue team must have gone by now, but every day he could hear voices and footsteps as people crossed above him. He was terribly weak. He had lost all sense of time and spent the days and nights listening for sounds above and fitfully dozing. But there was a stubborn streak in Freissegger, and he had no intention of giving up without a fight.

Firstly, he cleared the snow from around his left arm. With two arms free he worked at the snow tightly packed round the rest of his body. It was slow, painful work clawing away with his finger nails. In his weakened condition he could only work for a few minutes at a time, then he fell back, exhausted. He heard voices above him again. He shouted, but the footsteps plodded on, becoming fainter and fainter. He returned to his digging, but the amount of snow he managed to scratch away with his nails was pitifully small. By the eighth, or was it the ninth, or tenth day, he succeeded in freeing his trapped legs. They were swollen and white as the snow around them and were quite useless. He prodded them, but there was no feeling at all. He turned his attention to the snow above him, firmly pushing to the back of his mind any thought of how long it would take him to scratch his way through several metres of hard snow. He doggedly continued digging. Later,

he came across a piece of broken wood. Now he had a digging tool. Heartened by this he redoubled his efforts. The amount he dug out increased tenfold, but still more important, his piece of wood gave him the incentive to keep working.

When his initial enthusiasm wore off, he was left very weak and his progress became much slower. He heard voices again and more shouting, but once again the people carried on.

His diet of frozen snow was beginning to tell on him. He was now painfully thin and the ominous rumblings from his stomach were becoming more frequent. Time meant nothing to him at this stage, so he had no idea when it was that he first noticed the faint greying of the darkness above him. He dug on and the greyness slowly formed into a patch of light. He must be nearing the surface. Stubbornly he dug on inching his way upwards, then dozing for a short time. It took him hours. Suddenly his thrusting piece of wood met with no resistance, and an icy blast of air rushed in; he was through. 'Thank God,' he sighed with relief. Feebly he widened the hole and looked out. Dusk had fallen and soon it would be dark. He was bitterly disappointed. He collapsed know-

ing there would be no one about until morning. He had to spend another night in the snow. It would be too cruel if he were to die of exposure after all those days of killing effort. As he dozed off he wondered if it would be for the last time.

It had been light for some time and the party of men struggling up the mountainside could see their destination, the Winkelstation, standing out clearly against the snow.

'Help! Help!'

The leading man stopped, puzzled. He looked round, but there was nothing but empty snow in sight. Again, he heard the shout, feeble and hoarse; it seemed to come from the ground. Then they saw the hand. It was white and badly bruised and protruded from the snow and debris brought down by the recent avalanche. For several seconds they could only stand and stare wide-eyed. Then the incredible fact dawned on them; it must be either Gerhard Freissegger or Siegfried Lindner. It was midday of the 2 February, thirteen days after the avalanche, and the two men had long since been given up for dead. Carefully they began to dig Freissegger out. He was a frightening sight, more corpse than man. Skeleton-thin, his beard matted with frozen snow, he was tenderly lifted out, far too feeble to help himself. But his voice was clear and firm as he told his remarkable story. He could hardly believe that he had been trapped for thirteen days. By his reckoning he had been underground for at least two months.

By all rights Gerhard Freissegger should have been dead. Through indomitable will power he had survived, but at a fearful price. After a few days in hospital the surgeons had no choice but to amputate both legs at the knee. This would have meant the end for most men, but not Freissegger. Fitted with artificial legs, he was back at work by the autumn.

After thirteen days underground, Gerhard Freissegger is rescued, although more dead than alive

151

CHAPTER 15

Lone Atlantic Flier

*The next flash lit up
the cabin like day, and the
plane was tossed violently upwards.
Then it plummeted down and was flung
sideways completely at the mercy
of the raging storm.*

'Contact.'

The mechanic swung the propeller and the engine coughed into life. Taxi-ing forward, the brand new Lockheed Vega turned into the wind, and began to gather speed down the runway, its single engine flat out. As the lights of the airport raced past, the pilot looked at her watch. It was just 7pm, on the night of 20 May 1932. The slight figure sat tensed over the controls. She knew that she was in for a rough flight, but she was confident of fulfilling her childhood dream, to be the first woman to fly the Atlantic, solo.

At 34, Amelia Earhart, born in Kansas, was already a legend among American women flyers. Following in the steps of Amy Johnson, she was determined to show the world that women could fly as well as men. In many ways her career followed the same pattern as that of the English girl. Like Amy, her mania for flying came as the result of a 'joy-ride', when she went to see an aerobatic flying display at Toronto, given by an air.ace just back from the First World War. Amelia immediately took flying lessons, and by the following year she had made her first solo flight. A year later she scraped enough money together to buy her own aircraft, a rickety old biplane trainer, painted a bright yellow. It was in this machine that she really learned to fly. She practised incessantly. She also learned all the engineering necessary to carry out her own maintenance. In 1929 she entered for the California to Cleveland women's flying derby. Especially for the event she traded in her old biplane for an equally old Lockheed Vega. But a pleasant surprise awaited her when she flew the Vega to the Lockheed factory for inspection. The firm were so impressed with the way she handled such an old machine, that they exchanged it on the spot for a brand new Vega.

Amelia was fired by the exploits of Amy Johnson, and when, on 5 May 1930, Amy took-off from Croydon in a small grey-and-silver Gypsy Moth, to fly solo to Australia, Amelia, along with the rest of the world followed her progress hour by hour. The English girl had to make two attempts to take-off, for her little plane was so heavily loaded that it was difficult to get it airborne. She labelled her open cockpit, the 'Village Shop'. Crammed into it was everything that was likely to be needed on the long, gruelling flight.

Amelia preparing to set out on her long, gruelling flight

As she flew across Europe and on to Baghdad and Karachi, her attempt became world news. The flight took on all the thrills and excitement of an adventure story. Over India her engine began to cough and misfire; she had run out of fuel. Without hesitation she crash-landed her machine in a rock-strewn field near a native village, badly damaging one of the flimsy wings. This was quickly repaired for her by the combined skills of the village carpenter and tailor, who soon had her airborne again. Then, over Burma, the little *Jason* flew into a blinding

The tiny plane at the mercy of the appalling weather conditions. Inset: *Amelia Earhart*

monsoon. Battered and drenched to the skin in the open cockpit, Amy managed to crash-land on a Rangoon sports field, once again damaging the Gypsy Moth's wings. This time, students from a nearby engineering college came to the rescue, and she was soon off once more. Finally, over nineteen days after leaving England, and after a hair-raising experience flying over the shark-infested Timor Sea, she landed safely at Port Darwin, in Northern Australia. Fêted wherever she went, Amy won everyone's hearts by her modesty.

'Just call me Johnnie,' she would say, 'that's what my English friends call me.'

As the Vega took-off into the lowering clouds, Amelia began to have doubts. The attempt had been planned to coincide with Charles Lindburgh's historic flight in the *Spirit of Saint Louis*, but bad weather had delayed her start. At the first sign of a break in the weather, she had collected her maps, flying kit and two tins of tomato juice – all the food she was taking with her, and dashed to her aircraft.

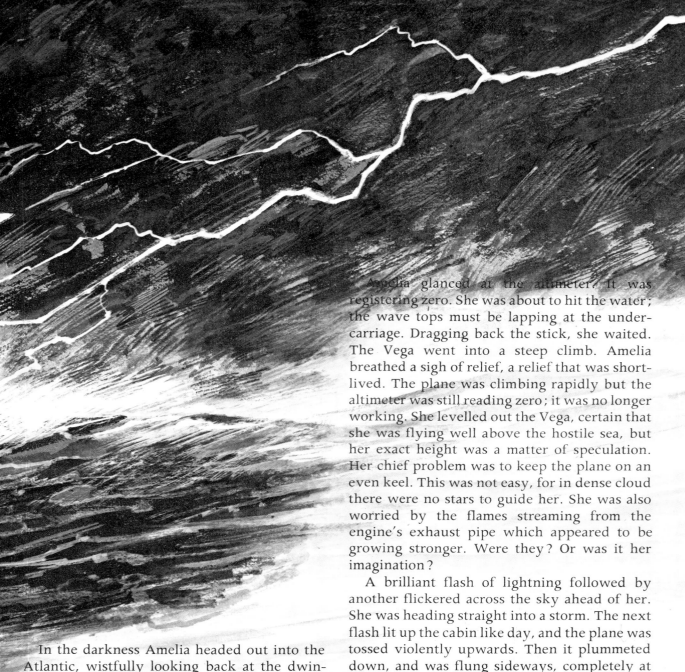

Amelia glanced at the altimeter. It was registering zero. She was about to hit the water; the wave tops must be lapping at the undercarriage. Dragging back the stick, she waited. The Vega went into a steep climb. Amelia breathed a sigh of relief, a relief that was short-lived. The plane was climbing rapidly but the altimeter was still reading zero; it was no longer working. She levelled out the Vega, certain that she was flying well above the hostile sea, but her exact height was a matter of speculation. Her chief problem was to keep the plane on an even keel. This was not easy, for in dense cloud there were no stars to guide her. She was also worried by the flames streaming from the engine's exhaust pipe which appeared to be growing stronger. Were they? Or was it her imagination?

A brilliant flash of lightning followed by another flickered across the sky ahead of her. She was heading straight into a storm. The next flash lit up the cabin like day, and the plane was tossed violently upwards. Then it plummeted down, and was flung sideways, completely at the mercy of the raging storm. Amelia eased back the stick; she would have to try to fly above it. In the pitch darkness the Vega began to climb, its wooden structure creaking and groaning as it was buffeted by the wind. Then the plane began to lose speed. The wings were icing up. She was forced to dive to avoid stalling, but she dared not descend too far with her altimeter out of action. For the next five hours, she flew blind through the dense cloud, wind and torrential rain, her compass made erratic by the storm.

In the darkness Amelia headed out into the Atlantic, wistfully looking back at the dwindling lights of Newfoundland. She realised only too well that the efficient working of the aircraft's compass alone stood between her and disaster. In 1932 there was no radar or sophisticated navigational aids, and should she run into fierce electrical storms, anything could happen. The Vega carried no radio so she would be unable to send out an SOS if she ran into trouble. The compass bearing appeared to be alright, but the dense cloud all around her was disturbing and the Vega was bucketing badly in the turbulent wind.

Dawn came as a relief. The Vega had weathered the storm, the white Atlantic rollers were hundreds of metres below, and miraculously she had stayed on course. But she only had a rough idea of how far she had come. She only knew for certain that she was well beyond the point of no return. It was then that she noticed the thin trickle of petrol leaking down the wing, close to the exhaust flames. If that caught fire, the Vega would go up in a sheet of flame. The possible alternative was nearly as bad. If she lost her fuel, it meant a forced landing into the sea. There was no sign of a ship; in every direction was an empty, grey waste. She decided that she would just have to fly on, and fly on she did. Her eyes were glued to the horizon ahead, but every now and again she glanced nervously at the leak and the fuel gauge. The leak seemed to be getting worse.

A long, dark smudge appeared on the horizon. Was it cloud or land? Gradually it became more distinct until she could make out the green hills and fields of Ireland. She had done it. Elated, she was tempted to fly on to London, but one look at the wing convinced her that she must land at once. The exhaust pipe had cracked, and flames were escaping from it, increasing the risk of fire. As she flew on she searched the ground below for a suitable landing place. At last she spotted a large, flat field, ideal for touching down, but as she circled it to come in up-wind, she realised there was a herd of cows grazing in it. She brought the Vega down in the meadow scattering the terrified herd. She leaned back. She was the

first woman to fly the Atlantic, solo, and in the record time of thirteen and a half hours.

Taxi-ing up to a group of startled farmhands, she stuck her head out of the cockpit and said simply, 'I'm from America'. From then on she was the 'Sweetheart of America'.

In May 1937, she took-off in an attempt to fly round the world. Her aircraft was a long-range airliner, a Lockheed 10E Electra. She was accompanied by a highly experienced Navy navigator, Fred Noonan. First, they flew down the coast of Brazil and then turned out into the Atlantic. 3,240 kilometres later they were flying across Africa on their way to Karachi. From Karachi they flew to Burma, via Calcutta, and on to Singapore and Java. On 30 June they left Port Darwin for Lae in New Guinea. From Lae they took-off for Honolulu by way of tiny Howland Island. Then the Electra disappeared without trace. A huge search was carried out by American ships and aircraft, over a quarter of a million square miles of the Pacific, but without result. Amelia Earhart was never seen again.

The farmhands and the cows are equally surprised to see their flying visitor